REALTOR RUB OUT

A LILY SPRAYBERRY REALTOR COZY MYSTERY

CAROLYN RIDDER ASPENSON

Carolyn Ridder Aspenson

DEDICATION

For Jack
My best friend and eternal Hottie Hubby

MESSAGE FROM
THE AUTHOR

Congratulations to Carole Craddock. She won the contest to be featured as the victim in Realtor Rub Out. She requested her character, which by the way, is not reflective of her personality, die with a cookie in her hand. And there, Realtor Rub Out was born.

To be notified of future releases and receive a free book, visit carolynridderaspenson.com

CHAPTER ONE

It's practically impossible to be a realtor these days. The competition is fierce, but the dead bodies, those really take a toll on potential sales; at least the dead bodies associated with mine and my best friend's firm, Bramblett County Realty.

That best friend and business partner, Belle Pyott, sobbed in my arms. "She was just…just lying there. I tried CPR, but she…she…it didn't help."

I patted her back. "I know. I'm sorry, Belle."

She sniffled as my fiancé and the county sheriff, Dylan Roberts, approached.

"Hey, how's she doing?"

I struggled to remove Belle's arms from their death grip around my neck. "Honey, you have to let go. You're choking me."

She dropped her arms and wiped her nose with a tissue Dylan handed her. "I can't believe this happened. I mean, it should have happened to you, not me." She blubbered loudly. "You know what I mean. I just don't have the stomach for this stuff."

Dylan and I shared a glance, and I mouthed, "Is Matthew coming?"

Matthew was a deputy sheriff under Dylan, as well as his friend, and he also happened to be Belle's boyfriend. I hoped his arrival would calm her. I'd never seen her so out of sorts, but I understood why. I wasn't an expert on finding dead bodies, but I'd experienced it more times than I wanted to admit, and it never got any easier.

"He's on his way."

Belle cried hearing that. Dylan raised an eyebrow and whispered in my ear, "I think she's in shock." He crooked his finger as he whistled to the paramedic. "Need some help over here."

The best volunteer paramedic in town, and a special friend to both Belle and I, Billy Ray

Brownlee, sauntered over, a fresh sweet iced tea and a Band-Aid in hand. Billy Ray always gave his patients sweet tea and a Band-Aid, and most of the time, that did the trick.

Except not with Belle, not that time.

"Oh, you're sweet Billy, but I can't. I'm sick to my stomach."

"It'll help you dumplin', it's good for that," he said.

Actually, the sugary, caffeinated drink was probably one of the last things she needed, but I wasn't going to burst Billy Ray's bubble or take away the thing he'd felt valuable for years. His heart was in the right place, and it wasn't about the actual drink anyway. It was the love he put into it that mattered.

Dylan handed me a Georgia driver's license. "The victim's name is Carole Craddock. You know her?"

I shook my head. "Not personally, but she'd emailed me recently about showing the property today, so I figured it was her." I gave him the license back. "What happened to her?"

He rubbed his chin, and I admired the slight five o'clock shadow beginning to show itself, even though it was only eleven o'clock in the morning. "No visible wounds, nothing showing she tried to defend herself. The blood around her mouth suggests poisoning, but we'll have to see what the autopsy shows."

Matthew walked in, quickly examined the scene and then headed straight to Belle, who started bawling in his arms all over again. He stepped outside with her.

"Why would someone poison her and how would they? I thought most poisonings were instant."

"Depends. Some take days or even months if the vic is given small amounts over time. Others can kill within minutes."

"Belle said she had a chocolate chip cookie in her hand when she found her, and no, we didn't touch anything, but do you think it could be that?"

He shrugged. "I don't know. We've got it bagged as evidence with the rest of the batch from the kitchen. We'll send it off today. If I put a rush on it, I'll probably know tomorrow or the day after at the latest." He rubbed my shoulder.

"I can't believe this happened. Again." I wasn't feeling sorry for myself, though Dylan must have assumed that. My angst was for poor Carole Craddock who'd died with a cookie in her hand and her entire life ahead of her.

"It's not your fault," he said.

"Of course it's not my fault. I know that. I'm upset because someone is dead, and she didn't deserve to die. Nobody deserves to die."

"Looks like someone feels differently about that."

I stared up at my fiancé. "We ask our clients to bake cookies before showings, or to at least leave them out. They could have done this." I hated to think that, but it was a possibility.

"We've already been in contact with them. They didn't know the place was being shown until they got the call from the realtor, and that was thirty minutes before she was scheduled to show up with her clients. Who, by the way, are MIA. The Studebaker's though, assured me they didn't leave any cookies."

"So, whoever did this came and left the cookies after the owners left and before the agent arrived? That's cutting it close."

He nodded. "Very close, but we don't know for sure if she got the cookies here, if she brought them herself, or if the cookie in her hand is what poisoned her in the first place. We don't have much of anything yet, but we will."

* * *

I showed up at Belle's place with a quart of cookies and cream ice cream and a bag of Oreos, my Boxer mix, Bo at my side. "Are you okay?" Bo's tailed wagged back and forth, smacking me on the side of my knee in a distinct pattern. I would end up with a slight bruise there for sure.

"I'm better," she said though her nose was stuffy and her eyes puffy and red.

I held out the sugary treats. "Girls' night?"

"You brought cookies and cream ice cream and Oreos? Is that supposed to be funny?"

I stared at the bag in my hand. "Oh. I hadn't even thought about that. I just thought my best friend needed some comfort food."

"Bless your heart for thinking of me." She grabbed two spoons from the utensil drawer and scooted into her family room, her footie slippers made a swiping sound on the hardwood floor. "I'm glad someone's come to sit with me. I'm sure Matthew's too busy to come by, what with having a murder to solve and all."

"Dylan said the scene's cleaned up already. Unfortunately, our listing is on hold for the time being, and the client is going to have to stay in a hotel, but it could be worse."

"Really? How?"

"Nothing was taken, and we don't have to solve some cold case to get a valuable family heirloom back?" I'd jokingly referenced a recent situation involving another listing of ours, but the effort didn't cheer her up, and it occurred to me it was probably in poor taste. "I'm sorry, that wasn't helpful." I'd hit two for two in the tactless department, and I hadn't even been there five minutes.

She stuffed a spoonful of ice cream straight from the carton into her mouth. "I appreciate the effort." She finished the scoop and leaned her head back on the couch. "How do you do it?"

"Do what?"

"Not see the image over and over again in your head. I keep seeing that poor woman lying there, that half eaten cookie in her hand, and the foamy blood on the corner of her mouth."

"You've been through this before, and you handled it better than anyone thought you would."

"Yes, but I was with a group of people before. It was different. I had to be strong."

"But you also spent time alone, and you survived. You made it through that, and that was someone you cared for."

"Twice is too much though. I don't think I'll ever sleep again."

"You will. You just learn to push the bad thoughts aside and focus on the good ones."

"How long until I find some good ones? All I can think about is what happened."

I took a bite of ice cream and contemplated my next comment. "I guess you just have to force yourself to think about something good and know that our wonderful significant others will figure out what happened, and they'll get justice for Ms. Craddock."

"But what if they don't?"

"They will."

She set the ice cream carton on her coffee table. "What if whomever killed her wasn't trying to kill her? What if they were trying to kill me?"

"Why would you even think that?"

"Because I'd planned to check on the property today, remember?"

"But how would someone know that?"

She shrugged. "I don't know. Maybe they overheard me talking about it? Maybe the owners mentioned it?"

"That doesn't make sense. Why would someone want you dead?"

"Because it was a Tuesday?"

"What?"

"Just because I don't know why doesn't mean someone doesn't have a reason. We learned that months ago during that decluttering and staging class. The reason could be something I did years ago."

I placed my hand on top of hers and tried to reassure her. "Nobody is trying to kill you, Belle."

"Maybe, maybe not."

CHAPTER TWO

Millie, the owner of Millie's Café, the best place in town for a good meal and a fresh cup of coffee or glass of sweet iced tea, filled a to go cup from a freshly brewed pot of coffee. "This should give you a big ol' energy boost. It's a new kind I'm trying. Got some extra lead in it." She smiled an unusually big, bright smile for the woman. I suspect it was because of her newfound old love Buford Jennings, a man that used to live in Bramblett.

I eyed the brown liquid and smelled its robust, nutty scent. "Better put a pump of sugar free vanilla in there just in case. Smells pretty strong to me."

She did as I asked. "How's Belle?"

"She's shaken, but I think she'll be okay. I stayed with her last night, but Bo slept next to her in her bed, so hopefully she got some sleep. Bo tends to be a bit of a bed hog."

"As big as that lug of love is, how could he not?" She handed me my coffee. "She going to work today?"

I nodded. "She's on her way here now. I left early to drop off Bo and gather my composure to help perk up her spirits. She was just so upset."

"You're a good friend, Lilybit."

"I try."

I sat at a corner table and sipped my coffee, but instead of thinking about ways to pick up my best friend's spirits, I selfishly thought about my upcoming wedding.

Dylan and I had worked hard to get to the place we were, and I didn't want anything to get in our way. Years together in high school and college, and then a several year separation to finally come back together again stronger than ever, set us on a path for a solid, strong forever and always, and I promised myself nothing would mess that up. To be honest, my biggest worry was the wedding, it had been since the beginning.

One part of me was ashamed for making things about me, but the other part said it was okay. I'd fussed and fretted for months about how to marry Dylan Roberts, and we'd finally decided on a destination wedding for close friends and family. But a murder investigation could take weeks, even months, to solve, and both my sheriff fiancé Dylan and his deputy sheriff Matthew couldn't, and wouldn't leave until they'd closed the case, and I wouldn't expect them to, either.

I had a choice to make. Wait it out and hope for the best or do a little investigating of my own. Since I had connections in the realtor world, and Carole Craddock was a realtor, I figured it wouldn't hurt to ask a few questions to help move the case along. Two birds, one realtor, so to speak.

Belle arrived later than I'd expected but had given me enough time to work through the beginnings of a plan. Millie offered to prepare her special breakfast for our distraught friend, who made it clear she couldn't stomach the thought of a two eggs over easy with hash brown potatoes and cheesy grits skillet, and asked for a muffin instead.

"Coming right up." Millie laid her hand on Belle's shoulder and squeezed. "You got this, sweetie. You're going to be fine." She headed back to the kitchen humming a happy tune.

"I definitely don't have anything, that much I know."

"It's okay. You had a pretty traumatic day yesterday, but I promise you'll be okay."

"You're a lot stronger than I ever realized. I'm not as strong as you."

"Are you kidding me? Let's revisit what I said last night about the decluttering and staging class murder, okay? You were a rock, and I don't think it was pressure, or support, or whatever, because other people were there."

She straightened in her seat. "I know. I thought about that while up most of the night with your snoring bundle of love. I did handle that well."

"Uh, yeah. I'd say so."

She raised an eyebrow. "Finding one dead body is hard enough, but two? That's more than I can handle."

"It probably felt different because you were alone. I think when we go through things like this with others, our defense mechanisms or maybe our egos help us handle it better, but when we're alone, our defenses are down, and we feel everything right away."

She nodded. "That makes sense."

Her eyes didn't have their normal sparkle, and the bags under them were swollen and puffy, but I hoped my idea would help put her on the path toward healing. "I'm going to make some calls and see what I can find out."

"About what?"

"About Carole Craddock. About where those cookies came from, and if they were meant for her."

She shivered and sipped on her coffee. "You think they could have been for me, don't you?"

"Nobody would have a reason to hurt you." Besides, I thought, the cookie in her hand didn't guarantee it was the cause of her death. Dylan had already made that very clear.

"You don't know that."

I nodded. "No, you're right, I don't know that for sure, but I'm pretty confident I'm not wrong about it. Either way, the best way to start an investigation is with the victim and her circle. If we can't find the killer in that, then we branch out."

"Investigation?"

"You know what I mean. I'll make some calls, see if I can find anything out, and go from there."

"You know Dylan's not going to like that."

I shrugged. "Hasn't stopped me before. Besides, he's my fiancé, not my boss."

"Oh my gosh, your wedding. What's going to happen now? We're leaving in seven days."

"Don't worry about that." I struggled to stay positive and keep my facial expression relaxed. "If Dylan and Matthew don't find the killer before then, I will."

* * *

I stepped through the double doors of Craddock & Clayton Realty and nodded to the young receptionist at the main desk. "Is Ms. Clayton in?"

The skinny blonde gave me a stern once-over, paying close attention to my dark straight-legged jeans and cotton pink button down. "Are you interested in buying or selling?"

"Both. I'm a realtor also."

The right side of her upper lip twitched. "I'm sorry. The agency isn't taking on new realtors at the moment."

I dug my heels into the tile floor. "I have my own agency. My name is Lily Sprayberry. I'm here to talk about the death at one of my listings yesterday."

"Oh, that was—uh, give me a moment please." She scurried to an office on the right and closed the door behind her.

As I waited, I gazed at the wall of realtor photos to my right and the long narrow table underneath filled with cookies, pastries, and two Keurig coffee machines with all the works for a homemade flavored latte. The office was much larger than mine and Belle's, with fifteen agents. Photos of Carole and her partner, Dabney Clayton, hung above them all.

I'd never met Carole, but she looked like a nice woman. In the professional looking photo, she'd pulled her long, light brown hair into a low ponytail that allowed her soft complexion and big brown eyes to shine through. I probably would have liked her.

"Ms. Clayton will see you now. Follow me."

Dabney Clayton was the spitting image of her photo. Shoulder length, whitish gray hair styled in the current angled bob style matched her creamy white skin–she'd brushed something sparkly and pink over—perfectly. Her fake eyelashes and thin dark eyebrows added pop to her pale complexion. Dabney Clayton wasn't someone I'd want to run into in a lit alley, let alone a dark one. It wasn't her appearance that sent chills up my spine, it was the stone cold, heartless eyes staring at me from the photo. I wondered if her clients felt the same.

She stood on the opposite side of her desk. "Miss Sprayberry. Please, sit."

When someone like Dabney Clayton said sit, people sat.

"What can I do for you?"

"First of all, I'm sorry for your loss."

She raised her left eyebrow. "Thank you, but I don't consider it a loss when a thief dies."

My jaw tightened. "You think your business partner was a thief?"

She set down her coffee cup and leaned back in her chair as she nibbled on a cookie. I'd seen the same cookies at the little coffee and snack station near the wall of photos. Chocolate chip ones, and they were homemade.

Her casual demeanor disturbed me. "Carole was taking our clients to a competitor. We had an agency together, yet she still thought it acceptable to move our clients to another without my knowledge."

"But you were aware?"

"I'd recently discovered. It was not something I expected."

"I see." I did understand that would be upsetting, however it didn't ring any *she deserves to die* bells in my barn, but that didn't mean another real estate agent's bells weren't chiming away non-stop. People did things for reasons I'd never understand.

"Clearly you must. Hundreds of thousands of dollars, Ms. Sprayberry. What ethical person does that?"

What ethical person wishes her partner dead? "Do you think that has something to do with her death?"

"Are you asking if I killed her?"

I stiffened. Dabney Clayton wasn't the kind of woman I'd want to upset. "No, ma'am. I'm simply asking if her alleged actions could have caused someone to harm her."

"Alleged." She waved her hand, and her attitude went from rude and agitated to easy going. "I highly doubt that. There isn't an agent in my office that could hurt a flea."

"What do you think happened then?"

"Well." She pressed her index finger to the bottom of her chin. "Let's see. Perhaps she also screwed the agency she filtered business to? Or quite possibly a competitive realtor had had enough of her shenanigans? Carole did have quite the reputation."

"Where were you around eleven o'clock yesterday, Ms. Clayton?"

"Are you inferring I murdered my business partner?" She tapped the tip of her pen to her lip. "My schedule is none of your business, Miss Sprayberry."

"Who was the agency she gave the business to?" She pressed lips together but didn't respond, so I tried another angle. "Can you think of who might be upset with her?"

She leaned toward the desk and kept her eyes focused on mine. "May I ask why you're asking so many questions, Ms. Sprayberry?"

I wasn't about to let that woman get my goose. I knew realtors like her, and though I wasn't as experienced, that didn't mean I was easily intimidated. I leaned toward her and stared right back into her scary eyes. "Your partner died in my client's home, Ms. Clayton. My clients expect me to keep them safe from situations like this. Finding out what happened in their home is my utmost priority." I leaned back and crossed my legs. "I have quite the reputation, too."

She blinked, and I knew I'd won that round at least. "Yes, well, if you want to talk to someone that Carole wronged, the list is long."

"Where would you suggest I start?"

She jotted a name on a piece of paper, ripped it from the spiral binder, and handed it to me. "Try this man."

"Thank you."

She scribbled a name on another piece of paper, ripped it off and handed it to me. "This one, too, though I don't think he's involved." She pushed her shoulders back and raised her eyebrow. "Now should any of my agents require questioning, I'd appreciate it being done by law enforcement." She stood. "I must get back to work. Carole's death has left me quite busy."

I stood too. "Thank you for your time."

I kept my shoulders back as I calmly walked out of the snooty firm, but when I was outside and out of their vision, I stopped the tough gal act. "Bless her heart. That woman is meaner than a snake."

Chapter Three

I sat in my car and searched the internet for the two names she'd provided. According to my GPS, Floyd Bowman, the man she said wasn't involved, had an office a short distance away, so I went there first.

Alpharetta Georgia had gone through a major transformation in the recent past. What used to be a typical small-town main street with mom and pop shops was now a booming upper middle class hot spot filled with trendy restaurants and microbreweries, expensive boutiques, and cigar bars. Off on the side streets were stacks and stacks of condo units and town home communities. It was a fun place, but it wasn't the small Southern town it used to be, and I had a feeling the people that had lived there forever weren't all that thrilled.

I pulled into the small public parking lot across from Floyd's office and parked. I checked my cell and read the four messages from Belle, responded, and then set out to see if Dabney Clayton had given me a real potential suspect or just tossed me a bone to get me out of her office.

"Well, hello there." Another perky, young receptionist greeted me as if she was over the moon with excitement about it. "Are you looking to buy or sell a home today?"

"I'm looking for Floyd Bowman. He was— he was recommended." It wasn't exactly a lie. At least that's what I told myself.

"Oh, Mr. Bowman is a wonderful agent." She whispered, "Probably my most favorite, but let's keep that between us."

I smiled. "Is he available?"

"He'll make time, I'm sure. Just a moment." She stood and sashayed to an office down the hall.

The real estate offices in Alpharetta must have hired the same interior designer. There were agent photos on a large side wall in

Floyd's, too, with his on the top, and underneath sat a table filled with similar cookies and baked goods as well as a Keurig. That office had a lot of money rolling in and out of it. I wondered why he had a problem with Carole Craddock.

"Hello." A tall, slender, balding man stepped out into the reception area. "I'm Floyd Bowman. I understand I come highly recommended to you."

I hadn't quite said that, but I reached out my hand and shook his anyway. "Lily Sprayberry. Actually, I'd like to talk to you about something important if you have a minute."

"Lily Sprayberry? I recognize the name." He turned around and told me to follow him.

His office was neat and orderly, and I envied that. Mine wasn't a mess, but it missed the tidy mark by miles compared to his. He asked me to sit at a small table in the corner, where he sat across from me.

"So, tell me why your name is familiar. Have I worked with you before? If so, I apologize. I have so many happy clients, I can't always keep track of them all."

"I'm a realtor in Bramblett County. Carole Craddock died in one of my agency's listings yesterday."

"What? Carole's–did you just say Carole Craddock is dead?"

I nodded. "I'm sorry. I just assumed you knew. She was supposed to show a property of ours, and when my partner went in to do a quality check, she found her. It was awful."

"I...I..." His skin paled. "I don't believe it. Carole?" He shook his head. "That's horrible. What happened? Heart attack?"

"The sheriff isn't exactly sure. They're waiting for the autopsy results."

"What? Are you saying Carole was murdered?"

"I'm not sure, but they're not ruling it out." I smiled. "Would you mind telling me where you were yesterday at approximately eleven, maybe ten thirty in the morning?"

He stood. "You think I had something to do with it, don't you? Who told you that? Skip Rockwell? Is that the high recommendation you told Allie I'd been given?"

That was a big, guilt ridden jump for him to take, and it set the hairs on my arms tingling. "No, sir." I apologized for the confusion. "Can you tell me what happened between you and Carole Craddock?" He hadn't told me where he was, but I didn't think I'd get it out of him if I asked again, so I didn't.

He placed his hands on his hips and leaned toward me. People liked to do that to try and intimated me. It didn't work, at least not anymore. "Why is that any of your business?"

"As I said, she died in my client's home. It's my duty to keep my clients safe."

That seemed to calm him a bit, but not as much as I'd hoped. "Carole…she…we…we used to work together. We competed. You know, challenged each other, but in a positive way. When we both left that firm, we made an agreement that we'd stay out of each other's way." He sat down again and sighed. "Only Carole decided to break our agreement."

"What do you mean?"

"Listen, I didn't kill Carole. I didn't even know she was dead, but I'm not surprised. Something happened with her. She changed. You're a realtor, I'm surprised you hadn't heard it through the grapevine."

"Bramblett is a small county. We don't get a lot of the gossip y'all do down here."

"Anyone worth their grain of salt knew to stay away from Carole. She'd steal a sale or heck, a client, right out from under you if you gave her the chance."

"Is that what she did to you?"

He nodded. "Pretty much. She was subtle about it though. Pushed her clients to make sales on homes pending contracts."

I flinched. "That's unprofessional and unethical."

"You're not the only one that thinks that. She wasn't always like that though. Only happened in the past year or so. I don't know what changed, but something sure did."

"Is that why would someone recommend I talk to you about her?"

"It was Dabney, wasn't it?" He rubbed the top of his head. From the looks of the shiny skin, he'd probably done that so much he'd rubbed his hair right off. "That told you to talk to me. She and I...we..."

I didn't agree or disagree. The entire story was interesting, and I just wanted to keep him talking. "What makes you think it was Dabney?"

"We have an agreement to keep each other informed about important things happening in the community. She probably sent you to honor that agreement."

That man lied like a rug, but I nodded anyway. "I appreciate your time." I handed him my card. "If you hear anything or think of anything that might be helpful, please give me a call."

He dug a card out of a card holder on his desk right quick and handed it to me. "Same, if you don't mind."

As he walked me out the front entrance, he stepped outside with me and said, "Ms. Sprayberry, I hope you don't think I killed her."

I nodded and walked across the street to my car.

Dylan sent me two text messages. "You up for lunch," and a few minutes later, "Don't tell me you're doing what I think you're doing."

That last one could mean a few hundred things, but I had a sneaky feeling he knew what I was doing and I'd likely be lectured when I talked to him.

Dylan wasn't a fan of my interfering with his investigations, but I considered my efforts more of the helpful kind rather than the interfering kind. After all, my addiction to TV crime dramas taught me a lot about sleuthing, and since I'd always wound up helping, I didn't see a problem with my efforts.

I connected my phone to my car and called him back while I searched for the address of the other person on the list, Skip Rockwell.

I knew Dylan would be busy with the investigation and likely not able to answer the phone, so I left him a voicemail. Sure, that was straight out avoidance on my part, but Momma always says there's a time to own up to your misgivings and a time to eat a slice of freshly baked apple pie, and I didn't have any pie, so... "Hey honey, I'm driving, so I can't text. Call me back when you have a minute. Love you."

I was ninety-nine percent positive he knew I'd gone to Carole Craddock's office, and if he'd gone there already, and Dabney gave him the same names she'd given me, he was definitely on my tail, so I had to move quick. Thankfully, according to my GPS, Rockwell & Associates was only three minutes away.

Skip Rockwell's firm was the exception to the rule when it came to Alpharetta realty firms. He didn't have a receptionist, nor did he have a fancy office with photographs of his agents on the wall. Instead, he chose the simple route, one similar to mine and Belle's. A large space with several desks, an oval shaped conference table, a small snack and coffee station, and an office along the back wall with windows looking out to the other desks—except we didn't have the office along the back wall. From the looks of the mostly clear desks, he only had two other agents, which was one more than Bramblett County Realty.

"May I help you?" A short, stocky man, weeks past the need for a hair trimming, stepped out of the back office.

"Are you Mr. Rockwell?"

He nodded. "What can I do you for, ma'am?"

"I'm told you know Carole Craddock. Is that correct?"

"Yes, ma'am. Every agent in town knows Carole. She do you wrong? Seems to be her thing these days."

A young man a few inches taller than Mr. Rockwell and with similar facial features walked into the office. "Hey, Dad." He introduced himself and shoved his hand out to shake. "John Rockwell."

I didn't give my name. "Nice to meet you."

"Here's the closing docs from the Harris sale. I've got a possible listing I'm running to. Be back after lunch." As he rushed to the door, he flipped around and said, "Nice to meet you, ma'am."

"Carole was found dead in one of my listings yesterday."

He blinked. "Oh heck, that can't be good for business. What happened? Heart attack? Woman was strung tighter than a harp."

"I understand you two might have had some conflict?"

He blinked again. "Conflict? No, no. Carole and I were good friends. Close. In fact, she'd just decided to come on board here at the agency. We hadn't signed the agreement yet, but she'd already been working with a few clients on the agency's behalf." He offered me a seat at the conference table. "Wait. Are you saying Carole was murdered?"

Was Skip's firm the one Dabney Clayton thought Carole funneled business to? I couldn't help but wonder why Carole Craddock would leave what appeared to be a successful agency where she'd been a partner, to come to something like Skip Rockwell's, but it wasn't my place to assume anything. "It's not been confirmed, but I've got a contact at the sheriff's office that seems to think that's the way the case is going."

"I...I don't know what to say."

I knew my time was limited. If I was right, and Dylan knew what I was doing, he'd send Matthew or another deputy out right away to stop me. So, instead of treading cautiously, I just went for it. "What was your schedule like yesterday, Mr. Rockwell?"

He pointed at his chest. "You think I had something to do with her death?"

I kept my gaze steadied on him.

He raised his hands and flipped them toward me, palms up. "I...I was with clients most of the day. I sell homes, and that's how we sell them, spending time with our clients."

"Were you in Bramblett County at all?"

"Bramblett County? That hole in the ground? You kidding?"

I wanted to kick him in the shin, but I kept a straight face and stood. "Thank you for talking with me."

He stood, too. "Sure, anything I can do to help Carole. Can't believe she's dead. We got a few clients we're working with. I'll have to give them a heads up."

Yeah, I bet he'd do that.

CHAPTER FOUR

"You do know this is an active investigation, right?" Dylan's tone wasn't as pleasant as I'd have hoped.

"You do know my best friend found a woman dead on the floor of our listing, right?" My tone was equally unpleasant.

He breathed heavily into his cell phone. "Are we going to spend the rest of our life together with you interfering in my investigations?"

"Think of it as me assisting you in solving crimes. It sounds much better that way."

He sighed again. "Lily Bean, we're getting married in a week. If you want me to make it to the altar, I need all eyes on this without any interruptions, okay?"

"That's perfect. I just had an eye exam two weeks ago, and my eyes are in tip top shape."

"I'll close this thing faster if you keep your beautiful eyes out of it."

Aw, that softened my resolve a bit, not enough to figure out what happened in our listing, but a little. "I've got the eyes of a goat."

"I can't disagree with you on that."

"I think Dabney Clayton is up to something. She wasn't at all happy with Carole."

"Yes, she made that clear. I can take it from here though, okay? You've got a wedding to finalize anyway."

"If it even happens."

"If you let me do my job, it will."

I had no intention of interfering with him doing his job, and I reiterated that, but I couldn't help offering my opinion. "What I found most interesting is that Carole Craddock was an agency owner, yet Skip Rockwell said she was going to work with him."

"Why is that interesting?"

"Because from the looks of the agency, it was successful, and Skip's didn't strike me as a booming business."

"That is interesting. Maybe she saw an opportunity to build it into something better?"

"Maybe. Just seems strange to me."

"I'll keep that in mind."

"See, I'm helpful. I'm not an interference."

"You're a good catch."

"Gee, glad you feel that way."

I'd been back at the office for most of the day, researching poisonings as well as agents in Fulton County, Georgia while Belle kept herself in high gear doing everything she'd planned for the next month in one day.

"I finished reorganizing our filing cabinets. Did you know we've got four hundred client files? When I matched those up with our newsletter, sixty seven of them don't get it, so I'm sending them emails asking if they'd like to subscribe. I've created a coupon for a free thirty minute home staging lesson if they sign up."

"And who do you plan on doing those lessons?"

"You, obviously."

"Oh honey, you're a hot mess."

She fell into her desk chair. "I don't know why this is bothering me so much. I mean, yes, it should bother me, but I've seen a dead body before. I just can't get past this."

She really was struggling because Belle wasn't the type to repeat things over and over unless she couldn't come to terms with something. "This is different, sweetie. Like I said, you were by yourself, just going about your normal life, and stepped into something you never expected. I felt the same way with Myrtle Redbecker. It's okay to struggle with it. Someone died. That's not something we just accept and then move onto the next thing."

"You kind of do that though."

"Not at all. Why do you think I stick my nose where it doesn't belong? Trust me, Dylan would be thrilled if I could move on."

"There's a lot riding on this though. I'm sure he knows that." She twisted a strand of her beautiful hair around her finger and sighed. "Then again, even if there wasn't, you'd be all over it like gray on a biscuit."

I laughed. "Maybe I should be marrying you instead of him."

"Oh, heavens no. You're far too high maintenance for me."

We both laughed.

"Look at this." I angled my laptop her direction, but she still had to scoot her chair to my desk to see the smaller print. "Craddock and Clayton was the top agency for three years running in Fulton."

"I knew her name sounded familiar, so I checked that when Bo snored—all night by the way."

"Did you see that it wasn't the top agency for 2018?"

"Yeah, so?"

I flipped the laptop toward me again and tapped into the Safari search bar. "Look what agency was."

"Rockwell & Associates."

"I spoke to Skip Rockwell and he said Carole was unofficially going to work with him, that they'd all but signed the deal."

"Really? For when?"

"I'm not sure. I just assumed it was recent, but maybe it's been happening for a while, and she was sending business to him and getting a cut of the commission or something?"

"Don't you think she'd get a bigger cut from her own agency?"

"I can't imagine she wouldn't."

"Then why send it over to his?"

That's what I wanted to know.

Belle flipped the laptop back toward her and scanned his website. "His site really needs an update. If I were looking for an agent, I wouldn't chose him based on this."

I nodded. "Something isn't right."

She tapped on my keyboard. "There's an agent lunch scheduled for that new mortgage broker in Alpharetta tomorrow." Her fingers danced over my keyboard. "I just reserved us each a spot. We might be able to get some info from someone."

"You go, girl."

"I'm always up for a good lunch."

* * *

I picked Bo up at doggy day care, and even though his tongue hung close to the floor and he didn't have a ton of energy left for me, he greeted me with kisses, which of course, I adored. We climbed into my car but skipped a trip to the dog park. Bo was a big hunk of love and always working to please, and sometimes I thought he pushed through his exhaustion to do just that, and I didn't want him to feel forced to play because of me. We drove home with his head on my lap snoring like a race car.

I had a habit of writing out details in both a notebook and on index cards, so I grabbed a stack of cards before I left work to use at home. It helped me organize my thoughts and sometimes see things with a different eye.

After feeding Bo and taking a quick shower, I made myself a pimento cheese sandwich, poured a tall glass of iced water, and hit the couch with my notebook and cards.

I created a card for everyone I'd talked to, as well as the victim and the homeowners, and laid them out on the coffee table in front of me. I scanned them, wondering if I should add another card, one I didn't want to, but did because I hadn't had a reason to rule the name out as an intended victim. I set Belle's card next to Harold and Shirley Studebaker, the homeowners.

Seven cards. Four potential killers. Four people that could have killed Carole Craddock, but by no means the only possible suspects. Real estate agents, if they were good, made friends or at least acquaintances, with everyone they could, and took every opportunity to leave an impression. There was no way to know if Carole had upset someone else, or honestly, if Carole was even the intended victim.

If she wasn't, then that left three options.

Harold and Shirley Studebaker and Belle.

Belle, my best friend since we were kids, and my business partner for the past few years. It was possible she was the intended victim like she originally thought, but that just didn't ring my probability bell. Belle was well liked in town and people adored her. But the truth was, one could never really know what might drive someone else to do something terrible like murder, and I had to consider that.

I sent her a text. "Don't take this the wrong way, but have you been ugly toward anyone lately?"

"I know what you're thinking," she responded. "And trust me, I've tried to figure out if I have, but for the life of me, I can't think of anyone."

Before I had a chance to respond, another text appeared. "Do you think the killer was trying to poison me?"

I really didn't, and I didn't want to worry her any more than she already was. "I don't think so, but it's important to consider all angles."

"That's what I told Matthew."

I typed back a quick reply. "What did he say?"

"He asked me a few questions. Couldn't come up with any reason, but probably because I'm lovable and couldn't think of a soul that felt otherwise."

I laughed, but I knew she was worried, or she wouldn't have made the joke. "I trust both of our men to keep you safe." I hoped that would ease her concerns.

"They are. He is. I have a special GPS tracker on my phone because he didn't want my location services on so someone can track me. He's got me checking in every time I go anywhere and when I leave. If he could, he'd have a deputy follow me."

"That's not a bad idea. Maybe they can put someone on you for added protection?"

"You know it's a small department, but after chatting with you at the office and exhausting myself trying to avoid the whole thing, I'm over it."

"Explain, please."

The little dots that showed me she was typing held on longer than normal, so I knew it would be a big response.

"Matthew's right, and so are you. There's really no way anyone could have known I was going to the Studebaker's, well, other than the Studebakers and you two of course, but I seriously doubt a couple in their eighties would want me dead."

"I agree." Relief washed over me. Belle's life at risk was scary enough, but Belle knowing her life was at risk and freaking out about it was harder to handle than the little pig my daddy brought home when I was six. And that cute little thing ran faster than anything I'd ever seen. "I honestly don't think it was meant for you."

"Neither does Matthew. He talked to Shirley and Harold anyway. He's diabetic, so they watch their sugars and don't even have cookies in the house."

I replied with, "Interesting," and added an index card under their names with diabetics under it.

Belle and I texted a bit more, but her texting fizzled off a few minutes later and I knew she'd likely fallen asleep. Like Bo, who was nuzzled up against my hip and snoring again.

I wished I could shut my eyes and be out like that in seconds, too. I gently pet his head, but he didn't budge.

I stacked the cards into piles, each with a possible motive or other relevant information, but none of them had much yet, though I didn't expect they would. And none of the possible suspects gave me any sort of alibi either, other than Skip Rockwell, whose was flimsy at best.

The one that concerned me the most was Dabney Clayton. In my highly unprofessional and moderately skilled—due to recent events only, not training—opinion, she had the most to lose, and the most to be angry about. She wasn't upset Carole was dead, and she didn't have a nice thing to say about her. I noted that on her main card and moved onto the next.

Floyd Bowman's motive wasn't nearly as strong. When it came to motive, I wasn't sure it even was one, but it was the best I could come up with.

He thought Carole was using her clients to steal sales out from under him. He hadn't offered any proof that she was, but I hadn't asked either. I'm not sure what I would have done in that situation, and bringing it up when the woman was found murdered might lead police, or people like me, to assumptions that did more damage than good.

As a motive, that would be hard to prove anyway because there was no way to know Carole had done that. Agents weren't legally allowed to offer information to anyone but the listing agent, and the listing agent could only share that offer with the sellers. Did we share the information anyway? At times, yes. Could I verify that every agent did that? No. I could only assume, and if anyone asked a group of agents if they shared that kind of information, they'd all deny it.

The only other ways Floyd would know would be if he was the listing agent who'd come to the home with a buyer, or if the buyer decided to tell him.

I would hedge a bet on him working both sides of the sale because most agents that listed properties also helped the seller find a new home, and if possible, would show homes in their catalog first.

The last possible suspect, Skip Rockwell, baffled me. He had no motive to speak of, or at least he didn't speak of any to me. Then again, I knew Dylan was on my tail, and I rushed our conversation, offended him, and very likely ruined my chances for getting anything else out of the guy. Recent situations though had taught me that if there was a motive, it would reveal itself soon enough.

I didn't consider my clients to be suspects, so I had to at least entertain the thought that they could have been the intended victims. But who would want the Studebaker's dead? They were harmless, and everyone in town loved them. At least that's what I thought. I circled each of their names and drew a question mark on each card and then clipped them together. My plan for the next day included a visit with the elderly couple.

I clipped the rest of the cards together, stuffed them and my notebook into my bag, and yawned as I pushed myself up from the couch. "Come on buddy, let's go to bed."

Bo opened one eye, grunted, and went right back to sleep.

CHAPTER FIVE

Bo stretched and yawned on his three-quarters of the bed as I pulled my tired body out from under the sheet. He closed his eyes again and was back asleep in seconds.

"Come on Bo, time to go potty."

After a minute or two of pets and snuggles, he finally dragged his big beige and white body out of bed and meandered like a window shopper in town toward the back door. I let him out and made myself a half pot of coffee.

Dylan walked in just as the coffee pot finished.

"Perfect timing." I gave him the cup I'd poured for myself.

He smiled and kissed me on the forehead. "Thanks. I'm definitely going to need a pot or two of this today."

"Long night?"

He nodded. "I thought I'd come by and we could share what we got from the agents you weren't supposed to talk to yesterday."

I smirked. "Sorry about that."

"No, you're not." He winked at me.

"You're right. I'm not." I finished pouring Bo's food into his bowl, let him in, and went to get my bag. I pulled out the cards when I got back to the kitchen. "Let's sit on the back porch. It's beautiful out."

We stepped outside, but I left the door open for Bo. Once he finished gobbling down his kibble, he'd be back out and energized to run circles around the yard.

"I've ruled out Belle as a possible intended victim."

"That's good."

"But I haven't talked to Harold and Shirley yet. It's possible they could be, especially if the cookies there were intended for them."

"Matthew spoke to them, but we aren't leaning that direction."

"But it's possible. It's their house. They're well known in town, so there could be someone upset with them, and it's easy to drop off cookies as a gesture of," I paused to think of a gesture, but couldn't come up with anything. "You know, just a gesture like neighbors or friends do." I sipped my coffee. "Maybe they upset a neighbor because they're selling their house? Or," I sat up straighter and pressed my palms onto my thighs. "Maybe they got in a fight with someone and that's why they're moving, and this person doesn't want them to just move, they want them gone."

He laughed. "The Studebakers are what, close to eighty? It's unlikely they've ticked anyone off in years. Lily Bean, when it comes to murder investigations, you can't create theories based on no solid information. Theories don't often solve crimes. Sometimes you've just got to go with your gut."

I smiled. "Aw, you're teaching me about investigating. Does that mean you want my help?"

He scooted his chair toward mine. "It means I know my fiancée well enough to know she's going to try and find the killer no matter what I say, and that I don't want to try and change her."

My eyes lit up. "So you're going to give me information on the case?"

He shook his head. "This is still a murder investigation. I can't share information with you, but I can offer you my thoughts." A smile crept across his face. "And you can share your information with me."

I clapped. "Oh yes! This is perfect."

"It also means you need to do what I say, and if I tell you to back off or not do something, you need to listen to me, okay?"

"Yes, sir, Sheriff. I'll do whatever you ask."

"We both know that's a lie."

"Is that what your gut's telling you?"

He nodded, and I giggled. "I'm my mother's daughter. Momma doesn't lie."

"Ask your father what he calls it then."

"I'm guessing he calls it embellishes. Momma embellishes."

"I thought that was a male character trait?"

I smiled. "Well, of course it is, sweetie, but it's also a Sprayberry trait, and it doesn't recognize gender."

We talked about the rest of the potential suspects, with me primarily focused on Dabney Clayton.

"She just gave me a creepy feeling."

"That's the gut thing I'm talking about."

"She said something about not feeling bad that a thief was dead and didn't have a nice thing to say about Carole. I mean, you can be mad at someone, but who really wants that person dead like that?"

"Her partner was stealing clients and handing them off to another agency. I can see how that would upset her."

"So, you think she did it, too?"

He laughed. "I'm not there yet, but I don't have the emotional connection to the business, so I may not see it as seriously as you do."

"Trust me, it's a serious accusation, but I'd never consider killing someone because of it."

"Remember what I told you before?"

I nodded. "Money does strange things to people."

"That's not exactly what I said, but you're right. It can drive people to murder. Good people, too."

"Do you have any suspects? Hypothetically speaking, of course."

"Hypothetically speaking, we have a small list, but if I was the sheriff, I'd do more digging before I arrested anyone."

"Yes." I nudged his arm. "If I was marrying a sheriff in a week, I'd tell him to do the same."

His smile sunk into a frown. "About that."

"Oh, no. No. No. No." I covered my ears. "I don't want to hear this. My gut is definitely telling me I don't want to hear what you're going to say."

He squeezed my knee. "We're still getting married. Matthew and I will make sure this case is solved before then, and if that means we have to come a day or two late, that'll be okay, right?"

I let out a long, worried breath. "Yes, that I can handle, but that's about it. We've waited a long time for this."

He stood and drank the last of his coffee. "Then it's time I get to work."

Bo galloped up to him and stood at his side, expecting something, which we all knew was a ride to day care.

"Bo, I'm taking you this morning, sweetie," I said.

"It's okay. He likes to ride in my squad car. He feels like a law enforcement officer in the front seat." He rubbed his ear. "Maybe, if he behaves, I'll let him hit the siren button."

I laughed. "With those opposable thumbs he doesn't have? Besides, you have a lot of work to do."

"It's on my way." He rubbed Bo's head. "And he's my guy. We like our boy time together."

A little something in my gut pinged, and my thoughts immediately went to what a good dad Dylan would be one day. "Then he's yours, and thank you for taking him."

He kissed me on the top of the head. "I already consider him mine." As I walked him into the kitchen and out the door, he said, "If you find out anything, let me know right away."

"Ditto."

He nodded, but I suspected that was just to appease me.

* * *

I made a pit stop at Millie's Café for a light but healthy breakfast because my cupboards were bare, and I didn't want to go to the grocery store before leaving for the wedding.

Millie greeted me with a hot cup of coffee and a warm biscuit with a touch of honey drizzled on top. "Hey there Lilybit. Haven't seen you in a while." She placed the small breakfast on a table and popped a squat in the chair next to the one I'd picked. "How's the wedding planning going?"

"That's not the right question."

Her eyes widened. "What's goin' on? That boy do something I need to get on him about?"

I laughed. "No, of course not. He's almost perfect, like always. It's not him." I took a bite of my biscuit. "There's been a murder, you know that."

She blushed. "Oh bless my ever lovin' heart, I forgot."

"Did you see that boyfriend of yours last night or something? Every time you see him, you're rattled for days." I smirked. "It's cute, young love."

Months ago when we'd found out an old friend of Millie's was living in an assisted living place in another county, Belle and I made arrangements for the two to see each other again. They'd had a thing years ago, and those sparks were still there. It made her happy, him happy, and all of us over the moon with excitement for her. Millie in love was like heaven on earth. She cooked better than we ever thought possible.

"He ain't no boy, that's for darn sure." She giggled. Millie, the toughest woman I knew, the one the entire town respected if for no other reason than they feared her–and she made the only good coffee in Bramblett County–giggled.

It was a rare sight, but one to definitely be seen.

"I spent the evening with him at the assisted living place. You know they don't know how to make gravy there?" She crunched her cheeks up and in toward her nose. "Worst stuff I ever tasted. I had to go back to the kitchen and have me a little chat with the cook. Kid's no more than twenty-five years old. Ain't no way that boy can cook a good pot of gravy. There wasn't even no tub of lard in sight."

Millie had owned the café for as long as I could remember, and it was the favorite pick for breakfast and lunch in Bramblett County. The food was typical Southern comfort food, made fresh, and served with an attitude. No one messed with Millie. She wasn't a crotchety old woman by any means, but everyone knew she had a switch the size of a small tree in her kitchen, and she'd whipped those into shape who disrespected the people she loved, or her food. Probably more her food than people, but because of the switch and all, no one said that out loud.

I laughed. "I'm pretty sure lard is a no-no at an assisted living facility, Millie. They try to be healthy in their food choices."

"They might could give them people something with some flavor." She shook her head and took a bite of my biscuit. "Why, I wound up making something for us, and half the residents wanted it, too. Ended up cooking dinner for twenty-seven people last night." She wiped her brow with a napkin. "I'm still give slap out from all the running around that big kitchen."

I could see Millie doing that, and I worried she'd over exerted herself. "You need to relax at night, Millie. You're going to drive yourself to an early grave doing that kind of thing."

She shrugged. "Don't think I'll be doing it for too long. Looks like I might have a roommate come next week anyhow."

My eyes popped open, and I almost jumped out of my seat. "A roommate?" I grabbed her hand and squeezed it. "That's the best thing I've heard in weeks."

She hesitated but then she smiled, and I could tell by the light in her eyes she was excited. "Buford's a good man, and he don't need to be in that place. We've been friends for years, and I got me an extra room that's sitting all but empty, so I figured why not?"

I giggled. It was sweet that Buford would move into Millie's spare room, or that's what they wanted the town to think. It wasn't my business, and I didn't much care what they did behind closed doors, just that they were happy. Millie deserved it more than anyone I knew. "I'm so happy for you. Does he need help moving? What about your place? Do you need anything done before his stuff gets there?"

"Sweetie, I appreciate you offering, but you got a wedding to prepare for, and I don't need you focusing on me. We got help, and we'll be fine."

Bonnie and Henrietta walked in just then, waving their hands and smiling like they'd been up to no good. Which was probably the case with those two.

"Hey, y'all." Bonnie pulled up a seat and sat next to me. "You talking about our little floozy here getting ready to shack up with a man she ain't married to?"

"He's renting a room from me you, and who you calling a floozy? You look in the mirror lately?"

"Why yes, I have, and I'm mighty easy on the eyes, if I do say so myself."

I chuckled.

They fought, but it wasn't a real fight. Each of them just liked to poke the bear every chance they got.

Henrietta had taken a seat next to Millie. "You got them boys scheduled yet?" She nudged her on the arm. "I could use me a little variety. Old Man Goodson and Billy Ray Brownlee are a little slow on their feet these days."

Probably because they're old men trying to keep up with an old woman that had the energy of a middle-aged one. "Henrietta, that's not nice. Those men would do anything for you and Bonnie." And they had. They'd switched girlfriends between the two women when asked for months, though I had a feeling that wasn't too hard on them. It was the other things that wore them out, things like running them around town, picking them up and sitting them on their laps, and the like. The men were too old to be acting like teenagers, but they loved every minute of it.

"Oh sugar, they have," she said, winking at me. "But a little variety is good for the eyes. I'm not asking for much."

Millie shook her head. "I got them scheduled, but I ain't telling you for when. I know you, and you'll have those boys running scared five minutes after they see you."

"What're you talking about?" I asked.

"College Hunks Hauling Junk," Bonnie said.

"Oh, the movers?" The company was a franchise with several locations around North Georgia. My clients used them for moves all the time.

Millie nodded. "I got me a discount because of my age, and they're coming to get some stuff out of my house to make room for some of Buford's stuff. I want him to feel at home."

"I bet you do," Henrietta said.

"Henrietta, hush," I said.

She smiled.

"I think that's a great idea, Millie, and they're a great company. I've had several clients use them. I think you'll be pleased."

She agreed, and when two more customers came in, she scooted behind the counter to take their orders.

"How's our Belle doing?" Bonnie asked.

"We brought her over some chicken soup last night and tried to cheer her up," Henrietta said. "She didn't look that good."

"It's hard going through what she did."

"Well, you ought to know. You're the expert on dead bodies," Henrietta said.

"Gee, thanks."

"Belle said they think the cookie was poisoned. That's a horrible way to die. Everyone loves a good cookie."

She was right about that.

"She should have smelled it first. Cookies got their own smell, and if it ain't right, I won't eat it," Bonnie said.

Henrietta raised her eyebrow. "You are the craziest person I know, smelling cookies."

Bonnie ignored her. "So, what's the plan? When we going to get to solving this case?" She pulled a package out of her large orange bag. "I got me and Henrietta here an investigator kit, and we're ready to start right now." She set the box on the table.

"What's an investigator kit?" Part of me thought it would be something helpful, but since Bonnie had purchased it, I didn't think it would be all that beneficial. It was probably an internet buy for kids, but I withheld judgement.

She opened the box with a Swiss Army knife she'd removed from her purse, too. I flinched when I saw that. The last thing Bonnie needed to carry around with her was a knife. Well, the second to last thing. The first was a gun.

She peeked inside and giggled with a whole lot of giddiness, and I knew it wouldn't help. "Oh, God bless the internet. This is perfect."

"Well, come on you old coot, show us what you got," Henrietta said.

She pulled out two small, plastic walkie-talkies and handed one to Henrietta. "This here's a gadget thingie we talk to each other through. You know, like them spies in the movies." She removed a thin, nearly flat silver item and held it up for all of us to gawk at and ooh about. "And this," she flipped it around in her hand. "This is a—I don't know what it is, but I bet it's important to catching killers."

Henrietta yanked it out of her hand, opened it up, and then showed it to each of us. "It's an ink pad. And an ink pad ain't gonna do us no good helping Lilybit and Belle figure out who made that batch of killer cookies."

Bonnie grimaced. "It sure will. All we gotta do is get a hold of one of them cookies, dust it with some flour from Millie's kitchen, get the finger prints off it, and then go and get the finger prints from the suspects. Like taking milk from a cow."

"Like you've ever even tried milking a cow."

"I don't think we can do that," I said. "I think it's probably some infringement of the suspects' rights or something, and I doubt Dylan would appreciate it. Besides, I'm pretty sure the ink would soak into the cookie, but what else is in the box?"

Bonnie grunted. "Y'all don't know how to investigate. My grandson Nicholas showed me how to watch movies on the Netflix TV thing, and I've been watching me a bunch of those British detective shows, and I'm learning all kinds of stuff."

Belle had walked in and heard Bonnie's mention of watching detective shows. "Oh heavens, you're like an older Lily." She gave Bonnie a hug from behind. "I'm not sure that's a good thing." She glanced inside the box. "Oh, what's that?" She pulled out a magnifying lens. "What's this for?"

Bonnie snatched it from her. "It's for investigating. We're gonna help Lily and you here solve that cookie murder, and the stuff in this kit here is going to help us do that." She returned the items to the box.

Millie stepped over, handed Belle a cup of hot coffee and then nodded her head toward the door while staring at me. "Your fiancé is headed this way, or at least someone from the Sheriff's Office is. Two coffee tumblers are waiting over on the counter for them. Must have been a long night."

"It was. He even told me he'd need a few pots of coffee. He must not have been kidding."

"I spoke to Matthew, and they really don't have much to go on at the moment. They should get the cookie results back today though."

We all knew Carole Craddock was poisoned. We just didn't know if the cookie was the actual culprit.

Matthew and Dylan walked into the café. Their tan uniforms, crisp and clean, fit like they were specially made for them, and they wore them well. I always got a fluttering of butterflies when I saw my fiancé in uniform. He hadn't had it on when he'd come by earlier, so I was surprised to see him in it.

I raised an eyebrow, and he knew what I was referring to because he smiled and whispered, "Public image and all."

"Good morning, ladies." Dylan attempted to peek into the box, but before he could get a good look inside, Bonnie slammed the flaps shut and put it on her lap.

"This here's personal stuff for our investigating job," she said.

I gritted my teeth. Dylan glanced at me, but I just shrugged. Deny. Deny. Deny. It wasn't a lie. I hadn't asked them to help, and Dylan knew those two women well enough to know nobody told them what they could or couldn't do. They just claimed they were too deaf to hear and did whatever they wanted.

"Is this something we should know about?" Matthew asked.

Belle held up her hands. "I've got nothing to do with it, I swear. I just walked in and saw the magnifying lens, that's all."

Millie had given both of the men a cup of coffee, and when Belle said magnifying lens, Dylan nearly spit his out. He squatted down next to Bonnie so he was eye level with her. Bonnie was as short as she was round, having gained a touch of weight over the past few months, and it suited her, because she was just as adorable as ever. "Miss Bonnie, you're not planning to interfere with our investigation now, are you?"

She smiled at him and kissed his forehead. "Sheriff, I promise you we won't do a thing to get in your way. I've been watching the Netflix, and I've got me a list of questions to ask your suspects." She opened her purse and took out a small spiral notepad. "Billy Ray is on his way here to take me over to the print shop so I can make you a copy."

Belle pressed her hand to her chest. We both knew Bonnie's intentions were good, but we understood the effort probably wasn't necessary.

"Ma'am, I appreciate your doing that for me, but how 'bout I just take a picture of the questions with my phone? That way you won't have to go to Forsyth County like that."

"Oh, you're a sweetie pie, Sheriff, and a good looking one at that." She placed her hand on his shoulder and whispered in his ear. "You ever want to dump Lilybit there, I can make myself available. I know how to shoot a gun, but you already know that."

Belle covered her mouth and faked a cough to hide her laughter. "Any news on the cookie?" she asked.

The men shook their heads. "Not yet, but it's early."

I checked my watch. It was early, but I'd planned a quick stop at the Studebaker's house and needed to get on my way. I had a busy day ahead with finalizing a few wedding items on my to-do list and figuring out what happened to Carole Craddock, not to mention a professional to-do list a mile long. Oh, and the broker lunch. I couldn't forget about that.

Weddings required planning I'd never imagined, and destination ones even more than I'd originally thought. What I thought would be easy ended up being a lot more work than expected, and I worried I wouldn't have things together before Italy or while there. If nothing else, I needed to have my work ducks in order before we left, and hopefully, the wedding would fall into place easily once I made it to Italy. If I made it to Italy.

But keeping my eye on the prize was important, and since Belle and I would both be gone, we'd lose a week of opportunities and possible clients, but we'd made arrangements to have an agent in Forsyth County take our calls, so at least there was that.

CHAPTER SIX

I drove to the Studebaker home, admiring
the two small goat farms along the curvy road
on the way. As a kid I'd ridden my bike to
those farms to play with the goats, and Belle
and I had practically broken our ribs from
laughing at their screaming. I slowed as I
passed each, waving at the herd of goats as I
passed. When things settled down, Belle and I
would have to take a trip there and play with
them.

Harold Studebaker answered the door shortly after I knocked. Wearing a green and yellow striped, long sleeved button down shirt and a pair of pajama bottoms, the scruffy bearded man blushed when he saw me. "I don't normally answer the door half dressed, but my wife is in her knickers at the moment."

"Oh, it's okay. I'm immediately in my jammies the moment I get home, so I always answer the door in them."

He smiled. "What can I do you for young lady?" He stepped to the side to allow me in. "Can I get you an iced tea? It's been in the sun for three days now. Ripe with flavor."

"Oh, that would be nice, thank you." I'd learned a long time ago if someone offered you a drink, take it. It allowed you to stay longer, and if you needed to close a deal, you just drank the drink slowly. I figured I'd get the drink in case Shirley Studebaker took her time getting dressed.

Harold Studebaker brought me back my drink and set it on the table in the family room. "You hear about that woman I assume?"

"Yes, sir. I'm sorry that happened here. We don't usually have situations like that."

He nodded. "Seems to me dead bodies have a way of showing up around you, but I understand. Means God's callin' on you to do good work."

I hadn't really thought of it that way. I liked that concept a lot. "Well, if he is, he's sure making me work hard now, isn't he?"

He chuckled. "We all have our gifts, Miss Sprayberry."

"Please, call me Lily."

Shirley Studebaker hollered from the bedroom. "Harry, is that Lilybit?"

"Sure is honey. Came by to talk about that woman that went to the Lord here."

"Did you offer her a coffee or tea?"

"Yes, ma'am."

She stepped out from the bedroom and into the hall, taking a look our direction. "Good. I'll be out right quick. Just finishing getting ready for the day."

Shirley Studebaker wore blond wigs, had for as long as I could remember, and she'd yet to put one on. I pretended not to notice. "No rush, ma'am." I smiled at Harold. "Mr. Studebaker, I understand you're diabetic?"

He nodded. "Part of getting old, I guess. Shirley's got to give me a shot before I eat, but it's okay. Don't bother me none."

"So the cookies obviously didn't belong to you?"

"No, ma'am. We know we're supposed to put them out for visitors, but they're too temptin'. I love me a good cookie."

I understood that. I loved me a good cookie, too. "Mr. Studebaker, is there anyone that can get into your home? Someone that has a key perhaps?"

He pursed his lips and furrowed his brows together to a point at the base of his nose. "Let's see. Our kids do of course, but they ain't been in town for months. Little Harry Junior is living in Alabama now, and his sister Emmajean's up in northern Tennessee."

Shirley Studebaker walked into the family room and sat next to her husband on the couch. "Neither of them were here." She smiled at me. "Already told that nice police officer that, too."

"I'm just trying to figure out what happened. I don't want things like this happening with our clients, and if something we're doing puts you in danger, we need to fix it and do our best to keep you safe."

"Oh heavens, sweetie, we ain't in no danger," she said. "We've been living here too long for that. If someone wanted to hurt us, they would have done so by now."

"Is there anyone you think might want to hurt you, Mrs. Studebaker?"

"'Course not."

"You know, Mr. Ronnetti, he likes cookies," Harry said.

"Mr. Ronnetti?" I asked.

"Joey. That's our handyman. Comes by a few times a month to fix things for us. Harry here can't do it no more. His fingers are a knotted mess. He's got that arthritis bad now."

I nodded. "Was Mr. Ronnetti here recently?"

"Yes, he was. Just the other day he stopped by, and I told him we had a leaky faucet in the hall bathroom. Said he'd come back and take a look at it."

"He's always got a lunch box with him, full of cookies. Used to sneak me one or two," Harry said.

"Probably part of the reason I'm sticking you like a pig every day now to test your blood sugar."

He blushed. "I haven't had me a cookie in months, honey. I promise."

She gave him a death stare, and I held back a giggle. They were adorable, sitting next to each other, his balding head barely higher than her crooked blond wig. I hoped Dylan and I would be that happy at that age.

"Did you tell the deputy about Mr. Ronnetti?"

Harold shook his head. "Didn't think of it till just now. I might could make a call and let him know."

"It's okay. I can call him." I sipped my tea. "Do you think Mr. Ronnetti is upset with you about anything? Could something have happened that made him angry?"

They glanced at each other, but only in a *do you know something I don't know* way, and then they both shook their heads.

"Don't think that's the case," Harold Studebaker said.

"Does Mr. Ronnetti have a key to your house?"

"Oh, no, 'course not. But he knows we leave one under the pot on the front side of the garage, next to the porch. Had that there since the kids were little, even though we never locked our doors back then," he said.

"Would you mind giving me his number? For the sheriff. I'm sure they're going to want to talk to him."

While Mrs. Studebaker stepped into the kitchen to get it, Harold and I made small talk.

A few minutes after she returned, I'd finished the last of the sweet tea, which really was delicious. "I'm sure the sheriff will have this case wrapped up soon, but in the meantime, Belle and I were hoping you weren't upset we had to pause the listing on the home. We just want to keep you safe."

"Oh, it's okay. The deputy said the same thing. We was planning on callin' you today to make sure it was off the market for now," Shirley said.

"I'm sure they'll solve the case quick though, so you shouldn't have to worry. In the meantime, if you need anything from us, please just call. We're happy to help."

They saw me out, and I called Dylan the minute I got in my car. I left him a voicemail with Mr. Ronnetti's information, and then I checked online on my phone to see if I could locate his business or residence.

It wasn't that hard. He had a small online presence that included his address. I put it in my GPS and headed to his house.

I was familiar with the area on the outskirts of the county, but I hadn't met Mr. Ronnetti, which was unusual. I'd assumed I knew almost everyone in town. In fact, I'd worked hard to do that. It was good for my business. I hadn't thought to ask how long he'd been working for the Studebakers, and I wondered if it wasn't long. It couldn't have been if I hadn't yet met him.

Mr. Ronnetti wasn't home, but his wife was. A short, stocky Italian woman that reminded me of a sweet grandmother, wearing a house coat and an apron greeted me with a big smile. She asked me to come in, and I accepted, but the thought of another drink made my already full bladder push back with a big, hearty no thank you. I usually did as my bladder said.

"I was hoping I could talk to your husband about some work for some of my clients. We like to have a few good handyman services on file for when we list properties."

"You can talk to my husband, but he won't talk back. God rest his soul, has been dead for years now. My son Joey took over the business after he died. Moved me here with him because he said the competition in Forsyth County was rough."

"How long have you been in Bramblett?"

"About a year now. But he's been working with the Studebakers for a few years. That's why you're really here, right? The murder?"

Busted. "In part, yes, ma'am."

"He's a wreck because of that. Doesn't want the police to think he had anything to do with it."

"Why would they?"

"Because he works for the couple, and he's got a record, but nothing serious. A few bar fights, a small drug charge. You know how boys can be, rough housing over sports. He's a Big Ten fan, but no one here cares about Big Ten football. It's all Alabama, Georgia, and Auburn."

That was true. I wasn't sure I could even name a Big Ten team, though I wasn't much of a football fan, other than the Georgia Bulldogs. "I understand your son likes cookies."

She laughed. "Who doesn't? And I make a mean batch of lemon cookies, his favorite."

The cookie in Carole Craddock's hand was chocolate chip.

"You don't make chocolate chip cookies?"

"Sure I do, but my boy's favorite is the lemon, so that's what I make him. Just made a fresh batch yesterday, too." She waddled into the kitchen and presented me with a plate full. "Have one."

The last thing I wanted to do was eat a cookie from a stranger. I wasn't sure I'd ever eat a one I didn't make myself again, but I didn't want her to think I thought she wanted to poison me. "Oh, no thank you. I have been on one of those no sugar diets. It's been hard, but I'm finally past the cravings." I said a quick prayer asking God for my forgiveness for the little fib.

"Why you young girls do that to yourselves makes no sense. You want a cookie, you should eat a cookie. God's going to kill you whether you're a stick or a tub. If it's not one way, it'll be another. You should just live your life."

Her point was valid, but just in case, I still refused.

"You think my son had something to do with the dead woman, don't you?"

I sighed. "Honestly, I don't know what to think. The sheriff doesn't even know what happened to her. They're waiting on the tests to find out her exact cause of death."

She smiled, but I could tell it was more forced than genuine. "I know my boy didn't have anything to do with that woman's murder. Why would he? And I don't mean to sound like I don't think my boy is smart, but he never did all that good in school, and plotting a murder, that's a little too much for him to think through."

I laughed. "I think I'll take a cookie after all. To go, if you don't mind."

She wrapped two in plastic wrap. "I'm giving you an extra for the police."

I smiled. "You're a wise woman, Mrs. Ronnetti."

"I'm Italian, I've got good intuition, and it's telling me you're barking up the wrong tree."

I raised an eyebrow. "Do you have a tree you suggest I should bark up?"

"I come from a big family. I've got uncles that were involved in the mob back in Chicago. They always had three reasons to fight. Love, money and territory. You look into those three parts of the dead woman's life, and you'll find your killer."

"Thank you. I appreciate your help." I handed her my card. "Would you mind having your son call me when he's home?"

She nodded and closed the door behind me.

I drove the cookies straight to Dylan's office.

CHAPTER SEVEN

I arrived back at the office in time for Belle to meet me at the door while locking it. "I was wondering if you'd forgotten," she said.

I checked my watch. "Oh, the broker lunch. I did forget, and I reminded myself this morning about it, too."

"We can still get there, maybe a few minutes late, but those things never start on time anyway."

"You drive."

I filled her in on the cookie situation on the way.

"Do you think he could have done it?" she asked.

"I'm not sure. Dylan said I should go with what my gut says and not create theories, but the TV shows do a little of each."

"Dylan's a real cop. I'd go with what he says."

"But they always solve the cases quickly on TV."

"Bless your heart, you're becoming your mother more and more every day."

I laughed. "I consider that a compliment."

"You should, for the most part."

"So, here's what we need to do. I'll point out the people I talked to yesterday, and we can both kind of stick near them, listen to what they have to say, and see if anyone else is talking about what happened."

"You don't need to point them out. I've already checked their company photos."

"Look at you, you're already a sweet Southern detective."

"No, I'm a real estate agent. I just play detective when I find a dead woman in our client's homes."

"Twinsies."

"Not the thing I want to have in common with you." She checked her review mirror. "Look at that traffic behind me. This is why I don't ever want to leave Bramblett. Why, I'd pitch a fit a mile long and deeper than Hades if I have to drive in this mess every day."

"Honey, you pitch a fit if the person at the stop sign on Main Street sits for more than two seconds. I think it's more you than the traffic."

We arrived at the luncheon just in time to hear the new brokerage owner give his speech. I stood just a few feet away from Dabney Clayton. Belle was next to her on the right, and I hid on Belle's right.

She leaned into me and whispered, "Listen to his accent. Must be from New York City."

Belle thought everyone that wasn't from Georgia was from New York, but I could tell the accent was more Midwestern than East Coast. "I think he's from Minnesota or something."

She shrugged. "I can never tell."

After his speech, we sat at the same table as Skip Rockwell and his son, John. Dabney Clayton chose a spot across the room and near Floyd Bowman. I figured the agents with bigger businesses stuck together.

"We've met, right? At my office?" John Rockwell asked. "Don't think I got your name."

I nodded. "Yes, Lily Sprayberry." I angled toward Belle. "And this is my business partner, Belle Pyott."

They shook hands across the table. "Nice to meet you," he said. "John Rockwell." He placed his napkin on his lap. "Dad said you were asking about Carole Craddock?"

"Yes. She was found in one of our listings."

"By me," Belle said. "It was horrible."

His dark brown eyes softened. "I can only imagine. How are you holding up?"

"I'm okay. It was just hard."

"I bet."

"We're trying to find out what happened," I said. "We don't want this kind of thing to hurt our reputation, or for it to make our clients think working with us isn't safe." I hated the way that sounded, but I was horrible at speaking off the cuff, and it was the only thing I could think of to lead into my question. "Have you heard anything?"

His father leaned over. "Carole wasn't the best team player, but she knew how to make money. You ought to talk to her former partner over there again." He pointed to Dabney

Clayton. "She's been madder than a snake since she got here. Maybe she'll even tell you the truth this time."

John Rockwell agreed. "Dabney found out Carole was coming on board as a partner in our firm and flipped out. Accused her of stealing her for her clients."

"You can't actually steal a person from another agency. They choose to leave," Belle said.

"They can be given incentives to switch though," I said. "Is that what you did?"

"I don't make those decisions. I'm not a partner, just an agent. But I can tell you the man doesn't like change, so however he got her to come over, I doubt it included him doing anything different." He shook his head as if he was having an internal discussion with himself. "I've been trying to get him to make changes for over a year now, but he won't budge. He needs to get with the times, work social media more, that kind of thing, but he's old fashioned. We could be making a lot more cash if good old dad would take some risks."

Skip Rockwell laughed. "My son, always judging me for what he thinks I don't do, not the things I've done that've allowed him the life he's got." He glanced toward the other side of the room, waved over to another agent and excused himself, so I took the opportunity to dig deeper. "Mr. Rockwell, do you know anyone that might have an issue with Carole Craddock?"

He leaned back in his chair. "Call me John, please. Every realtor in town had an issue with the woman, and I think that's why my dad brought her on. She was a shark. Knew what to do to make the deal and didn't stop until she did."

"But you just said your dad didn't want to do things to increase business."

"Nothing I suggested at least. He doesn't think I've got a handle on how things work yet. Carole, he respected. Knew she was a snake, but if the snake didn't bite him, then he was good. I'm sure he gave her a sweet deal." He held up his hand and rubbed his thumb and fingers together. "One she couldn't refuse."

"Did you have any issues with her?"

He flinched. "Who me? No. I mean, yeah, sure. The typical ones anyone has with a—you know the kind of woman I'm talking about— but nothing big."

John Rockwell wasn't much older than me, so his attitude toward women was surprising.

I'd think someone our age would be a little more kind, at least in their word choice. Then again, it really wasn't the choice of words, but more his tone that put me off.

I excused myself from the table, and as I stood, I tapped Belle on the leg hoping she'd continue the conversation with him. I walked over toward the hallway for restrooms and stopped just at the start of it when I heard hushed voices and biting, strong tones. And the voices were ones I recognized.

"Did you see her?"

I peeked around the corner to watch Dabney Clayton and Floyd Bowman in a heated discussion.

"It's fine," Floyd said. "We don't have anything to worry about. Just calm down."

"Calm down? How can I be calm? Carole's dead, and the police are going to find out what's going on if that woman keeps sticking her nose where it doesn't belong. We need to take care of this ASAP."

Were they talking about me? I pressed my back against the wall and listened some more.

"We have nothing to hide, baby. It's all good. We're fine, fine. I promise you, nothing's going to stop us."

Dabney Clayton mumbled something I couldn't hear, and my stomach lurched from sneaking into their private conversation and hearing what sounded like two lovers arguing, most likely about something they didn't want others to know, but still, it wasn't exactly my business. I shook off the icky, because the thought of those two being lovers made my stomach twist, and I scooted out of their as fast as I could without making any noise.

And when I did, I bumped smack into Skip Rockwell. "Well, hey there again, Miss Sprayberry. I meant to congratulate you, but I forgot, so congratulations."

"For what?"

"Why, your wedding, that's what. I hear you're getting married soon."

"I uh, yes…I'm getting married next week."

"To that sheriff, right? Sounds like he's got his plate full at the moment. Murder is tricky business. Sure hope nothing gets in the way of your nuptials."

"I can assure you nothing will get in the way but thank you."

"Well now, I wouldn't be so sure of that. You never know what might happen."

"What is that supposed to mean?"

"Just wouldn't want you putting yourself in danger or anything just days before your wedding now."

"Is that a threat, Mr. Rockwell?"

He smiled. "Have a nice day, ma'am," he said and walked away.

I marched over to Belle who was sitting next to John Rockwell laughing. "Oh sweetie, you just wouldn't believe what this boy is telling me." She rubbed his bicep and squeezed. "The things these city agents do, it's just so silly." She giggled with her fake laugh so I knew she was up to something.

He leaned his shoulder into her. "Stick with me baby and you'll learn a lot."

I swallowed hard. "Hey, Belle, can I talk to you for a minute?"

"Just give me a sec, okay hun?"

"So, tell me, are you a Georgia fan or one of those other teams from that other state next to us?"

"Go Dawgs all the way."

She giggled, and my stomach flipped again. Belle could charm the pants off any man. Her sweet Southern drawl, her long, full eyelashes; she knew how to play it, and she played it perfectly when necessary. I just didn't like it.

After my little chat with John Rockwell's father, I didn't trust him or his offspring.

"Belle, can we—"

She held up a finger. "Just a few more minutes okay, sweetie? This man here, he's helping me improve my sales skills. He's going to own his daddy's firm one day, aren't you sugar?"

He smiled and winked at her. "That's the plan."

"Well, I bet it'll happen. I can feel it."

Skip headed back our way, and trailing behind him were both Dabney Clayton and Floyd Bowman. Tension rose up my back, settling in my jaw. I clenched my fists but quickly relaxed them. I didn't want to seem nervous, even though I was.

Skip pulled out his chair, but instead of sitting, just gripped the back rest with one hand and leaned in casually like he hadn't practically threatened me a few minutes ago. He nibbled on a chocolate chip cookie. "Well, well, looks like you two are hitting it off. Comparing industry notes, are you?"

"Just reliving our college days," John said.

When Floyd and Dabney arrived at our table, the tension level shot through the roof.

The side of Dabney's upper lip curled. "Not surprising, seeing the Rockwell men—if one can call them men—engaging with small-town agents."

Belle pushed out her chair and stood. "Well, bless your heart, you're stuck up higher than a light pole now, aren't you? I bet you make your momma proud."

Dabney Clayton lurched forward, but Floyd Bowman grabbed her wrist and pulled her back. "Don't."

John Rockwell stood too, but his attention was focused on Belle. "Don't bother with her, honey. She's just a bitter woman looking for something she'll never have. A real man."

Heaven help us. It was going to get ugly.

The snarl on Dabney's face grew bigger. "Did you grow up in a barn?"

"Nope, next to one though."

Floyd Bowman laughed. "If you think being around this guy is being around a man, you've got another thing coming." He pointed to John. "They may be a small firm, but they're snakes, and they'll steal your business while smiling in your face."

Skip let go of the chair and straightened his shoulders. "You want to talk about stealing business, you dirty little—"

I held out my hand. "Fellas, this is not the place for this. Please."

Dabney Clayton snickered. "What are you, the etiquette police? I've been to your little run down county in the woods. There isn't a lady in sight. Not one worth their weight in gold, anyway."

"Oh, you've been to Bramblett, have you? When was the last time you were there? You know we had a murder recently, right?" I asked. She'd made me angry, and I fully intended to have my say.

"You go, girl," Belle whispered in my ear.

"Are you saying I had something to do with my partner's death?"

"I'm asking when you were in my little run down county last."

She furrowed her brow and snorted. "I don't dirty my hands with this kind of behavior."

"You want to know who killed Carole, take a look at her new partner here," Floyd said. "He'll do whatever he can to get a bit of our business."

Skip puffed out his chest and growled. "I didn't kill Carole, and you know it." He stood with his legs spread apart and his hands on his hips. "But you? We all know you and your girlfriend here had something to do with it. Yeah, Carole was planning to partner with me. Had all kinds of plans to take my firm to the next level, but it didn't include stealing business. You two wrote the book on that, so don't be pretending you don't know what I'm talking about."

Floyd leaned into Skip's personal space. "You calling me a thief, Rockwell?"

People had begun to gather. Rubbernecking happened everywhere, and lately, I'd been in the middle of all the action, whether I liked it, or not. And I didn't like it one bit.

"I'm calling you a thief and a murderer," Skip said.

Floyd grabbed Skip's shirt, and John Rockwell jumped in to break up a soon to be physical battle. He yanked Floyd's arm and pulled it away from his father, then stood in-between the two. "Now, now. How 'bout we take a break and go to separate corners to cool off? No need to show everyone here our dirty laundry."

"Wait a minute," I said, deciding to take the bull by the horns. "Why don't you tell me why you think Floyd is a thief and a murderer, Skip?"

Floyd bowed up again, and Dabney grabbed his arm to calm him.

"We all know what happened when he worked with Carole years ago. He likes to call it a little good-hearted competition, but everyone knows the truth. He found out Carole's client made an offer on a property her client wanted, and he got one of his clients to bid higher on the property, and according to her, he kept doing that. Don't know how he found out about the offers, but he did, and every time she had a client ready to make one, he'd go in and grab it for one of his clients right out from under her."

I eyed Floyd. "Mr. Bowman told me it was the other way around."

"'Course, he did. Wouldn't want to make himself look bad now, would he?" Skip Rockwell asked.

"I don't pull the rug out from other agents, Rockwell," Floyd said.

Skip wiggled his finger between Floyd Bowman and Dabney Clayton. "Both of you are rotten to the core. Stealing business and marking up homes to make a bigger buck."

"You're the one that stole Carole from our firm. We were business partners, and you just up and took her from me," Dabney said.

"I didn't take a thing from you. She walked away on her own. Or was planning to until your boyfriend here decided to poison her."

Belle squeezed my shoulder. "We need to go. I need to get back to the office."

My cell phone vibrated in my pocket with a message from Dylan. "Coroner said the victim's stomach contents contained sulfate dioxin. It's slow acting, but definitely enough to kill her. Doesn't appear to be in the contents of the cookies left at the Studebaker's, so we're working on where it came from. Keep this between us, please."

I glanced at Belle. "Results on the—I mean, I need to get to the bridal shop. My dress is ready, and I need to pick it up." That was the truth. I'd had a voicemail earlier, and I wanted to stop there on the way back to the office since it was between counties.

"Oh, sweetie." She gave John Rockwell the biggest set of Southern gal ogly eyes I'd ever seen. "I have just loved chatting with you, but bridezilla here must be attended to, and I have got to get away from the tension in the room." She patted his bicep and gave it a light squeeze then stared at the other three agents. "Why, it's just so thick you could cut it with a knife."

He brushed her black hair away from her face, and I thought it would be a heck of a night for her if Matthew discovered her little act. Part of me wanted to be there to watch her dig herself out of the hole she'd created, but the other part knew that could end up bad for both of us. "There's some tension in the room all right, but I think it's of a different kind."

Ick. My stomach couldn't leave that one alone and got itself all up in knots.

As we drove to the bridal shop, Belle's general mood sat somewhere over the moon but south of entering a new universe all together. "That was amazing. Did you see how I finagled that guy? He thinks I'm an idiot."

"And that's a good thing?"

"I played him, and I'm sure he would have told me what he knew if those idiots hadn't ruined it."

"If he knows anything. John Rockwell seems like the kind of guy that says what he thinks, even if it's not exactly the truth."

"Maybe, but it's more than we have now, right?"

"Maybe not." I filled her in on my conversation with Skip Rockwell.

"Oh, that's creepy, especially the being threatened part."

"I know. I think he's hiding something, and now I'm just more confused."

"Sounds like we might have our killer."

"I don't know. They all kind of threw each other under the bus just now." I adjusted the seatbelt so it wouldn't slice through my neck. "Besides, I'm pretty sure Floyd and Dabney are lovers."

She cringed. "That's icky, but Skip did reference something to that effect."

"That's exactly what I thought." I went over their conversation with her.

"Oh, I like how you played that, all sneaky and detective-like. We are pretty darn good at this, aren't we?" She smiled over at me. "Sugar?" She smiled as she said that.

I laughed. "Bless your heart, you're becoming a stereotype."

"If you've got something that works, you might as well use it."

I preferred using questions and information to put together the pieces of the puzzle. Belle, it seemed, just liked to fly by the seat of her pants. "So, you know what this means right?"

"What?"

"That we've got three possible suspects that are all up to something."

"And I may be able to use John Rockwell to find out what they're all up to."

"Matthew isn't going to like that."

She pulled into the bridal shop parking lot and shut off her car before facing me. "My best friend is supposed to get married soon, and if this case isn't solved, there's no way her fiancé and his best man are going to get on a plane and fly all the way to Ischia, Italy. I'm not opposed to doing whatever it takes to make sure they're both on that plane." She grabbed her purse from the backseat. "Well, not whatever it takes, but darn close."

"And I appreciate that."

"I'd hope so." She closed her door. "I'm willing to step out of my comfort zone and get comfy with a slimy guy for you, and that's saying a lot. You know how much I detest slimy guys."

"Probably just as much as I do."

The salesclerk went into the back area to pull my dress as I stepped into a dressing room to undress.

Belle stood outside and chatted while I put on my gown. "You're still planning to ship our dresses to the hotel, right? We're not taking them with us, are we?"

"Yes, I mean, no. I mean yes. I called and they said they would keep it if we had to change our plans, or I could make arrangements to ship them back here if necessary."

"Let's hope that's not necessary."

I opened the dressing room door and stepped into the main area with the mirrors.

Belle gasped. "Oh my gosh. I...it's...you're...I just don't know what to say. You're beautiful. Just gorgeous." She crouched down and fluffed the small white pearl beaded train. "I knew it was a stunning dress, but I had no idea how perfect it would look on you." Tears welled in her eyes. "Oh, bless my heart, I'm going to be a hot mess next week." She walked a circle around me admiring the heart shaped neckline and the way it accentuated my shoulders. "Those spin classes have really paid off."

"You mean the ones I haven't taken in months?"

"Honey, you are the most beautiful bride I've ever seen, and we were in a sorority, so I've seen my share."

I laughed. "Well, you're supposed to think that. You're my best friend."

"Do you have a necklace picked out? That heart shaped neckline is perfect for something, and pearls would match the gown."

"I have a few options, but nothing that screams, *wear me* just yet."

"I'm sure you'll find something perfect. You know, I'm so glad your parents are going to your wedding. You mother would pitch a fit if she missed seeing you in this."

A tear fell from my left eye. "Stop it," I said as I wiped it away. "You're making me all emotional."

"You're getting married, you should be all emotional. When it's my turn, I'll be a hot mess, I'm sure."

"No, you'll be bridezilla, for sure."

She hugged me. "Hush."

We both laughed.

Belle slipped into her maid of honor dress, and I understood how she felt seeing me in mine. The long lavender gown fit her like a glove, which was exactly my intention in picking that particular style. The neckline was heart shaped to match mine, and it accentuated her curvy figure perfectly. Belle wasn't a gym rat, as people liked to call committed exercisers, but she was blessed with a figure to die for. I would have been jealous, but even though she was perfect in every way to me, she had her own psychological body image issues to deal with, like most women my age.

"Wow. If you ever get married, you definitely need a dress in that style. It's perfect on you."

She grimaced. "If I ever? You say that like it'll be a miracle if it happens."

"It's going to take a strong man to keep you happy, that we both know."

"And Matthew's doing a fine job, so that must say something good about him."

"Are y'all talking about getting married?"

"It's come up a time or two, but nothing serious."

"Then we had better make sure to keep our flaps shut about your little flirtation earlier. I don't want to cause any ripples and increase the odds of you being a spinster."

She laughed. "Honey, that man is wrapped around my little finger almost as tight as you've got Dylan wrapped around yours."

I smiled and fluffed the bottom of her dress as she walked so we could see how it laid out. "I bet you do."

"You don't have to bet on that."

CHAPTER EIGHT

A small box sat outside our office's front entrance. Belle jumped when she saw it. "Oh look, we got presents!" She grabbed the box as I unlocked the door. While I set my things down and ran to the bathroom, she opened the box. I returned to her staring at a piece of paper. "This isn't good."

"What?"

She handed me the paper and I read it out loud. "Mind your own business or you're next." I glanced inside the box and at a wrapped plate of chocolate chip cookies. "Don't touch those."

"I'm not crazy," Belle said.

I dialed Dylan's number. When it went to voicemail, she called Matthew as I texted Dylan, "9-1-1."

I checked the video and alarm system but yet again, neither of us had thought to turn it on in days, so it wouldn't do us any good in identifying who'd left the package.

Dylan responded that he'd be right there, and we assumed Matthew would come with him since he hadn't answered Belle's call.

Five minutes later, while we sat and stared at the box, afraid to do anything else really, they arrived.

"We touched it, but not after we saw the cookies," I said.

"Good," they said in unison.

They put on gloves and Matthew checked the rest of the office though we told them the door had been locked, and it was unlikely anyone had gotten in.

"All clear," he said.

"Told you," Belle replied.

Dylan examined the box closely as I took photos of it. "No postage, so it was dropped off at the door."

Belle crossed her arms and exhaled. "Do you think it's from the person that killed Carole Craddock?"

"Has to be. No one knows it could have been a cookie."

Dylan peered directly into my eyes. "Unless you said something."

"I don't think so. Wait, I might have to the Studebakers, but they're harmless, and when I talked to Joey Ronnetti's mother, she guessed, but I didn't say it."

"She guessed?"

"Well, I casually mentioned that I'd heard her son liked cookies, then I wouldn't eat one she'd made, so…"

He smirked. "Anything else I should know about? You might have ticked off the killer and he or she is trying to make a point."

I pressed my lips together. "We went to a broker lunch, and a few unexpected things happened."

"How about you tell me about them?"

"I might have been sort of threatened by Skip Rockwell, and there might have been a verbal altercation between him, Floyd Bowman, and Dabney Clayton."

Dylan removed his hat and rubbed the top of his head. "Sort of threatened?" He paced in a short line. "I don't know why I thought it was okay to let you in on this investigation."

"You what?" Matthew asked.

"He didn't exactly let me in on it. I kind of pushed my way in."

Dylan flung his hand at me. "You try and stop her. Woman's as stubborn as a mule."

"I think he just called you a jack—" Belle giggled but stopped herself from finishing that sentence.

I raised my eyebrows. "It was a broker lunch. We go to those all the time." Okay, we didn't go to them all the time, but once every six months wasn't never, either. "And I found out that there's some kind of romantic connection between Floyd and Dabney. I bet you didn't know that, did you? And by the way, if one of them isn't the killer, then they're up to something else that I'm guessing is illegal."

I let them know why I thought that.

"Did they see you spying on them?"

I blanched. "I wasn't exactly spying. I had to use the ladies' room and they were in the hallway having a disagreement. I didn't want to disturb them."

He smirked. "So, while you waited for them to finish you figured listening in would be a good idea?"

"Sounds about right," Belle said.

"You're not doing me any favors," I whispered. "Dylan, they're up to something. Dabney specifically mentioned me, or it sounded that way, and she's concerned."

"What exactly did she say?"

"Something like, the police are going to find out what's going on if that woman keeps sticking her nose in our business or where it doesn't belong. I'm not sure which, but it's close either way. I may be wrong, but it sounded like she was referring to me."

"Of course she was," he said.

"Wait a minute. Didn't Skip Rockwell say something about Carole being poisoned?"

Belle nodded. "Oh my gosh, he did."

"How would he know that if he wasn't involved?" I asked.

"Are you sure you didn't mention the cookies to any of them?" Dylan asked.

"I'm sure."

He stared at Belle with a raised eyebrow.

"Oh, nope. Not me. I didn't say a thing about any cookies."

"Looks like we've got ourselves a murderer," Matthew said.

"This is why I want you staying away from active investigations. Sticking your nose into them always gets you in some kind of trouble."

"But she's got the cutest little nose, Dylan, and you should see her in her wedding dress. You're going to burst a blood vessel at how beautiful your bride is."

His snarl softened. "I'd like to make sure she's still around for me to see." He walked over and took my hands in his. "If you're going to do this, please do it with a little distance between you and the suspects."

I nodded. I was a bit shaken by the cookies. Shaken for both Belle and myself. Whoever sent them knew we were nosying around in the murder investigation, and they weren't happy about it. And only the killer knew how Carole Craddock died. The killer and all of us. "I'll do my best."

He kissed my forehead. "Thank you."

Matthew wrapped the box in plastic wrap and dropped it inside a black string bag. "If you want cookies, you're going to have to stop at Millie's."

"We are totally fine with that," Belle said.

"You ready to arrest someone?" Matthew asked Dylan.

"Looks like we've got some more investigating to do," he said.

"Well, you all get to it. The sooner you solve this, the better I'll feel about sending my momma and daddy on a plane to Italy before me," I said.

"If we're going to keep getting little gifts like this, I say you send them now and include us in on the early arrival," Belle said.

Matthew pecked her on the cheek, and as they walked out, Dylan pointed to the security camera and said, "Turn the thing on now, will you?"

"Praise God for keeping my nose clean in that hot mess," she said after they closed the door behind them. "I thought I'd have to say something about my conversation with John Rockwell. He may be a slime ball, but I don't think he killed Carole Craddock. He's too worried about making a name for himself at his dad's firm. Which is kind of funny, considering you said it's not all that in a pair of tight jeans."

I laughed because she used a saying my momma used all the time. "Maybe he didn't kill her, but he might know if his father did."

CHAPTER NINE

Joey Ronnetti called me on my way to pick up Bo from day care. "This Miss Sprayberry?"

"Yes, and this is?"

"Joey Ronnetti. My ma told me to give you a call about the Studebakers."

"Oh yes, thank you for calling."

"I didn't kill that woman if that's what you're asking. Mr. Studebaker can't have sugar. Poor guy's a diabetic, so I don't offer him my cookies anymore."

His mother obviously told him what she knew. "Mr. Ronnetti, I've got to run and take care of something, but I'd like to come by your house after if you wouldn't mind?"

"Don't see a problem with that. You hungry? Ma's making a pot of spaghetti and meatballs, and she's going to want to feed you."

I thanked him and said I'd be there within the hour.

I grabbed Bo and fed him a few treats from the bag I kept in my car and headed to the Ronnetti's house. I didn't think Joey had anything to do with the murder, but I knew it was important to talk to everyone, so I wanted to follow through. Besides, he could have been there and seen something.

He was right. His mother offered me dinner, and the sauce smelled delicious, but I refused. I'd heard rumors about refusing an Italian woman's food, and they were right. Mrs. Ronnetti pushed and pushed, even when I told her I had a wedding dress to fit into in a matter of days. "Just a meatball then. You're too skinny. You need some meat on those bones."

I ate a meatball, and God bless that woman, it was one of the best things I'd ever tasted, so I had another, tighter wedding dress aside.

"Did you go to the Studebakers the day of the murder?" I asked Joey.

"No, ma'am. I stopped by there to check on them mostly, but Mrs. Studebaker mentioned a leaky faucet, so I said I'd drop by in a day or two, but I haven't made it there yet. Heard what happened by calling them and letting them know I'd be coming by actually, and then Ma here said you came by to talk about it."

I nodded. "Mr. Studebaker said you used to give him cookies."

"Yes, ma'am. Ma here makes a mean lemon cookie, and Mr. Studebaker, he likes them. Hasn't had one in a while though because of his diabetes. Mrs. Studebaker is small, but you don't mess with those country women. They're tough."

"Not as tough as us Italians," his mother said.

"Have you ever heard anything that concerned you while you were at their house?" I wasn't sure what to ask, and that was the first thing that came to mind. "Maybe they mentioned anything about a neighbor or someone they'd upset?"

He took a minute to respond and then said, "Not that I'm aware of. Don't think those two could upset a fly though. They're as nice as can be."

I glanced down at the plate and desperately wanted to lick the remaining red sauce from it because it was that incredible, but my momma taught me manners, and I just couldn't do it.

I smiled at Mrs. Ronnetti. "I'm going to come by and learn how to make this one day. It's the best thing I've ever tasted."

"You do that. I don't have a daughter to share my recipes with, and Joey here, he's never going to cook. I'd love to pass them onto someone."

* * *

Bo had been lounging on the screen porch with a meatball of his own and had licked his plate clean. I was jealous. He lay next to it snoring away, and both Joey and his mother laughed when I had to shake him awake. "His buddies at doggy day care exhaust him."

"Wish I'd had a place like that for Joey when he was a kid."

"Ma. I wasn't that bad."

"You weren't an angel either."

I laughed. Their relationship made me miss my parents, and I was looking forward to seeing them soon.

Or at least I hoped I'd see them soon.

I retrieved my index cards and notebook and made a few notes about the day while Bo—as usual—snoozed next to me.

Floyd Bowman and Dabney Clayton had something they didn't want people to find out, and specifically, me, or at least I thought it was me. What could that be? I tapped my pen on an index card when my cell phone dinged with a text notification from an unknown texter.

"Don't let Dabney Clayton fool you. She's not any better than Carole Craddock was."

"Who is this?" I responded.

"Dabney isn't innocent."

"Do you know something? Who is this?"

I waited a while and when I didn't get a response, hit info to call the number, but it sent me to a general voicemail for Craddock & Clayton. I wrote the number down on a separate index card just in case and copied the text message exchange word for word.

Did Dabney kill Carole? Was the anger she felt toward her soon to be former business partner enough to drive her over the edge? I thought back to what Dylan always said, and to what Mrs. Ronnetti said.

There are few things that drive someone to commit murder. Money, love, and territory. As Dylan said, passion and money. Mrs. Ronnetti added the third reason, territory, and I liked it. As far as I could tell, Dabney had two out of three reasons, money and territory.

Floyd Bowman said Carole manipulated his sales by going in and offering a higher bid, but Skip Rockwell said it was the other way around. If Floyd was being honest—a factor I had no way of proving—then he had every reason to be upset. But if Skip was right, he had less of a reason.

And let's face it, men aren't generally bakers. Sure, some men liked to cook, but most threw a few burgers or some barbeque on the grill and that was it. Actual baking was the exception to the rule.

But something about Floyd and Dabney's conversation made me wonder. What could they be hiding? Their relationship? I drew a big circle around Floyd's name on his card. I noted their conversation on each card and then also detailed out the text I'd just received on Dabney's card, too. It felt like double the work, but keeping the cards connected, I thought, could be the key to my wedding happening on time.

I shuffled the cards around, trying to figure out the biggest and best motive. No matter how I arranged them, Dabney Clayton kept taking the number one spot. She hit all the marks, and even some marks I hadn't thought of, like betrayal as a possible motive. I would feel betrayed if Belle gave her business to another firm, so it would be understandable if Dabney felt that way, too. Would that be enough reason to murder Carole, or was it just another piece of the pie?

I sent Dylan a text asking if he could come by after work, even though it was late. He responded and said he was just leaving and would. I felt bad because I knew he was exhausted, but I wanted to share my thoughts and get his input.

"I bake," he said as I explained my theory. "And I'm pretty good at it, too."

I'd sampled some of Dylan's baking efforts. I patted his back. "You might ought to stick to the grill, sweetie."

He chuckled. "We can't rule out suspects just because the weapon might be cookie. If someone wants to murder someone else, they're going to do what they have to do to be successful."

"But when you put it all together, you should consider it."

"True, and Skip Rockwell doesn't seem like the type of guy that sits around and bakes at night to relax."

"I agree, but Dabney? That's a different story. She falls into two out of the three motive categories, too. Money and territory, and if you add betrayal, she's there, too."

"Territory?"

"Do I have to teach you how to investigate now?" I winked. "Mrs. Ronnetti, she's Italian, and she said there are three reasons a person is driven to murder, at least it's been her experience."

"Her experience? How many people has she murdered?"

"Stop it," I swatted his arm. She wouldn't hurt a flea, but she's Italian, and she said she's got family members that were in the mob, and they always had three reasons to kill people."

He raised his eyebrow. "And what were those three reasons?"

"Love, money, and territory. Territory isn't always a location, it's an attitude."

"She didn't mention honor?"

"No, why?"

"Honor is a biggie with the Italians. Capone had a lot of men killed because of it."

"Honey, this is Bramblett County Georgia. We're a long way away from anything like Al Capone."

"Let's hope."

"But you see? It works both ways for Dabney Clayton. The money of course, but also, the territory. Carole was leaving her partnership with Dabney and taking her clients to another firm. That's territory right there if I ever saw it."

"She has an alibi, and so far, it's checked out."

What's her alibi?"

"She was preparing to show a house in Milton."

"Did you talk to the clients?"

He nodded. "They said they were with her around eleven o'clock."

"But you don't have a specific time for the murder yet, do you? Did you get the autopsy back?"

"We know that Carole died around ten thirty-ish."

"That's a thirty-minute difference. A lot can happen in thirty minutes." I showed him the text messages. "Maybe you should dig deeper. Maybe she took the cookie from the office?"

He focused on the message, took a screenshot and then sent it to his cell phone via text. "Did you try calling the number?"

I nodded. "And it went straight to a general voicemail box for Craddock & Clayton. Which means whoever made the call had set their calls to come from the main line at the firm. Someone that wanted me to know Dabney's not innocent."

"Or someone that wants you to think she's not."

"Like Skip Rockwell?"

"Or Floyd Bowman."

"Not possible. They've got something going on, he and Dabney, and I just don't think it's him."

"Whatever's going on can't be that important to Dabney. She's the one that gave us, and you, his name as a possible suspect."

He was right. "Probably because she wanted to deflect the blame from herself."

He agreed. "If she killed her, she'd want to redirect our investigation."

"Are you set on it being Skip Rockwell? Did you bring him in for questioning?"

"I'm not set on anyone just yet, and honestly, I don't see a motive for Skip. What did he have to lose in bringing a seasoned agent with a book of business on board? More importantly, what could he gain from killing her?"

"Her entire book of business for himself."

"But she hadn't officially transitioned over, and could he even have access to any of it now that she's gone?"

"It's possible. If he has access to her client base on her computer, or he could do a property search through the city of Alpharetta, but that would take a lot of time. Months probably."

"We have her computer. It was in her vehicle. We have a lot to find out still. We're interviewing agents from Craddock & Clayton, and we could have another suspect by the end of the day tomorrow. We just don't have any strong evidence for any arrests yet."

Which meant the odds of making it to Ischia for the wedding were getting lower by the minute, and I was determined to make sure Carole Craddock's murder didn't stop us.

CHAPTER TEN

All eyes were glued to me as I walked into Craddock & Clayton. I wanted to wave and gush at my popularity, hoping it was for my choice of professional attire–a black skirt that hit just above the knee, a pale pink silk button down top with three-quarter sleeves, and a pair of pale pink pumps I'd picked up the week before. I bought them because they were a perfect match to a sundress already packed for my wedding. They were a little pricy and over my budget, but they were cute as a bug on a rug, and I just couldn't say no.

I grabbed a donut from the table of food and took a bite out of it. "I love me some powdered donuts." I held it up and smiled at it. "Is this from a bakery, or does someone here make all of this?"

No one answered, and it was obvious they weren't gawking at me for my cute outfit. They did it because they feared Dabney would pop a screw loose when she saw me. And they were right.

"What in the…what are you doing here? This is my place of business, and I don't need you here fussing around things that have nothing to do with you."

"Mrs. Clayton, it has everything to do with me. Your partner was murdered in my client's home. It is my duty to them to find out what's going on, and I think you know more than you're saying."

She grimaced, flipped around, and headed toward her office. I stood waiting for the go ahead, and when she glanced back to check, she stopped and said, "Well, come on. Let's get this over with."

"At the broker lunch yesterday, before the altercation, I went to use the restroom, and I heard you and Mr. Bowman talking. You said you were worried about something a woman was sticking her nose into. And you mentioned the police." I sat in the chair in front of her desk. "You don't have a lot of friends here in the agency, do you?"

She flinched, and her face heated to a shade similar to the fire trucks in Bramblett. "You listened in on our private conversation?"

"Not intentionally, no, but I'll admit that once I recognized the voices and confirmed it was you and Mr. Bowman, I didn't walk away."

"That's a breach of privacy. Nothing you heard will ever hold up in a court of law."

I wasn't aware of hearing anything that would require a court of law in the first place. "Happening upon a private conversation and not wanting to interrupt it isn't illegal, Ms. Clayton. But I can't help and wonder if there was something you'd fear I'd take to the police."

Her eyes shifted, and she hesitated before speaking. "We were discussing an employee of...a situation with an employee. It doesn't concern Carole Craddock, and therefore, it doesn't concern you, either."

"When I first met you, you suggested I speak to Mr. Bowman about his relationship with Ms. Craddock. Strange that you would throw your boyfriend under the bus like that, don't you think?"

If Belle was there, she would have cheered me on. I'd gone into full out crime drama TV mode and was proud of myself.

"He is not my boyfriend."

"Well, I don't know what y'all do in these big cities, but where I come from, when men get all touchy feeling and whisper terms of endearment, they're either trying to sell a used car, or you're knocking boots."

Dabney glanced out her office window into the main work area with all the agent desks. There were six people out there, two men and four women, and one woman, a petite, curly haired red head in an adorable green and blue sleeveless dress, caught her eye. The young woman immediately glanced down at her desk.

"Ms. Sprayberry, I find your comment highly inappropriate and extremely offensive. And what I do in my private life is none of your business."

"Maybe not, but Carole Craddock's murder is, and I plan to do everything within my power to find out who killed her."

She shuffled a stack of papers on her desk and sighed. "Very well, you do that, but leave me out of it. I have work to do."

I nodded, and as I stood to leave, I placed my hands on her desk, an intimidating move I'd recently seen on TV. My wrists shook ever so slightly from my nerves. "Ms. Clayton, what's your favorite cookie?"

She glanced up at me. "Not the kind that killed Carole, I can tell you that."

"Why do you think a cookie killed her?"

She hesitated for a moment. "Because, I...because that woman never left the office without a bag of cookies."

"So, you're saying she took cookies from here, ate them, and then died?"

Her jaw dropped. "No, I'm not saying that. I'm saying that Carole Craddock loved cookies, and I heard that was what killed her."

"Where did you hear that?"

"Let's just say I did the math. Skip Rockwell said yesterday that she was poisoned, and she's always got cookies with her. How does that add up to you?"

"It's a reach."

"Only because you're sticking your nose where it doesn't belong. Even the simplest of law enforcement officers like the ones you've got in your little backwoods county can figure that out. Now, if you don't mind." She flicked her hand toward the door. "I've got work to do."

I nodded and walked out of her office. As I passed the young woman in the cute dress, I smiled, but she quickly turned away. I kept my shoulders back, knowing if I'd done anything in that short exchange, it was set Dabney Clayton on notice. I strongly suspected she'd killed her partner, and I had every intention of proving it.

My ego inflated, and my step confident, I marched out of that office feeling like I could conquer the world. So, when I saw the note under my car's windshield wiper, I wasn't at all concerned.

And then I read it.

When you play with fire, you're bound to get burned.

My ego was the balloon, and the note, a sewing needle.

I stared at the note, trying to decide what to do. I peeked back into Craddock & Clayton hoping no one noticed my furrowed brow and pursed lips, but not one single person inside faced the window.

I hadn't really paid attention to the people in there, but did a quick assessment of them then, all but the girl in the cute dress, because every woman notices a good fashion choice, and made a mental note of what they looked like. From the back, at least.

Could any of them have walked out and put the typed note on my car windshield? Yes, absolutely, and I wouldn't have noticed, because I wasn't exactly paying attention. I wanted to kick myself in the shin for that, too.

I stuffed the note into my bag and headed to the one place I'd find solace and support.

Millie's.

Two of my favorite people in the world were there stuffing scones and coffee into their mouths like they hadn't eaten in months.

"You had this new scone Millie's got? Henrietta asked.

"It's better than a plate full of barbeque and an ear of corn," Bonnie commented.

"Slathered in salty butter, too," Henrietta said.

Bonnie nodded as she heaved another chunk of the tasty treat into her mouth.

The two women, upwards of an age I learned to never mention even though I wasn't exactly sure what it was, had been a part of the decluttering and staging class Belle and I'd taught some time back. It was an emotional time for both of us, and through it all, Bonnie and Henrietta were both comic relief and support. Since then they'd become important people in our lives and even bigger comic relief than either of us thought possible.

Sometimes though, it was a bit overwhelming.

Which was I why I didn't concern myself with their all black attire, consisting of cotton sweatshirts and sweat pants, the kind that had the elastic band at the bottom of the leg. I giggled at the black knit beanies though. It wasn't exactly winter, and their perfectly coifed hair styles would have mighty fine cases of hat head when they pulled those things off.

I sat next to them. "What in the devil are y'all wearing beanies for?"

Millie brought over a milk jug filled with sweet tea. "They're planning on protecting you from death by cookie."

I sat between the two women. "Protect me?" I made eye contact with both of them, and Henrietta bent down under the table. When she finally pushed herself back up, she had a blue plastic bat in her right hand.

"Yup, from death by cookie," she said.

Millie snorted. "What're you gonna do, beat the cookie out of Lily if she eats it?"

"'Course not," Bonnie said. She bent down and held up her matching bat. "We're gonna beat the butts of the person that made them, that's what."

"With a plastic bat." Millie said, chuckling.

"And we got our investigator kit, the one from the other day," Henrietta said. "We're all set to keep our Lilybit safe and knock a murderer out cold if we have to."

Bonnie placed her hand over mine. "We heard about them cookies that got delivered to your office and the note that came along with them. We don't want you and Belle getting hurt, especially with the wedding so close."

"I appreciate that, but we're fine. We made a commitment to staying away from all things not given to us by personal friends."

"That's all well and good, but we're still goin' to do what we're planning," Henrietta said.

Bonnie agreed. "And besides, we don't want these bats here to go to waste. Cost me close to fifteen big ones at the Walmart yesterday."

I searched my purse for my wallet. "I am not going to let you spend that kind of money on us." I dug the wallet out and handed a twenty to Bonnie.

Millie yanked it from her hand. "You can't take that."

"Why not? I got a limited budget, and she's offering."

I calmly took the bill from Millie's hand and handed it back to Bonnie. "I insist."

"She insists," she said.

"Can't argue with the bride," Henrietta said.

"This ain't about her wedding," Millie said.

Neither of the other two women had a retort for that because at the same moment Old Man Goodson and Billy Ray Brownlee walked into the café with matching black sweat suits and beanies. I thanked God for not having a sip of coffee going down my throat at that moment because I was one hundred percent certain I'd have spit it onto the table and the crumbs of the scones left on the plate sitting in the middle of it.

I needed to find out what new flavor Millie came up with before the rest of the scones disappeared.

Millie snorted again when she caught a glimpse of the two older men, affectionately known as the man toys of both Bonnie and Henrietta. "Where's the plastic bats?"

Each man held up a golf club, and my eyes widened.

"Don't need no bats," Billy Ray said.

"We got us some clubs at the Goodwill down in Dawsonville. Three bucks each," Old Man Goodson said, and then he winked at me.

I'd recently grown to have a different kind of respect for the fragile looking man with the heart of gold. I'd once considered him sweet and unassuming, and while he was still sweet, I'd learned he was a lot smarter than people thought. I respected that about him, too.

"I think the person that left the cookies is looking for short cuts." I pulled the note from my purse. "I just got this a little while ago." I set the note on the table, and Bonnie went for it, but I stopped her. "I shouldn't have touched it either, but I kind of had to."

Millie put on her reading glasses hanging from a beaded strand around her neck. "When you play with fire, you're bound to get burned."

"Well, they might could learn to spell burnt."

I didn't tell her that in that case, the proper spelling was actually burned.

"Sounds like a threat to me," Bonnie said.

"Glad we got us some weapons," Henrietta said.

Billy Ray held up his golf club and it shook in his hand. "Got all the protection you and Belle need right here."

"That's not going to be necessary." I tapped onto my phone's screen. "I'm texting the sheriff about it now."

"Ain't it cute how she calls her fiancé the sheriff?" Bonnie asked.

"He is the sheriff," Millie said.

"I know that, woman. You got to get that chip off your shoulder."

"I don't got nothing on my shoulder."

"Once she shacks up with Buford, she'll be nice again," Henrietta said.

I held back a giggle, but it was hard, because I kind of agreed with Henrietta on that one. "It's stressful, getting your house ready for another person. I'm going through it now." I was. Dylan would be moving in shortly after our return from our honeymoon, and I'd spent as much of my free time as possible making room for him and all of his man stuff, and believe me, he had a lot more stuff than I had time and space for, for sure.

"Don't mean she's got to be a cranky old bitty in the meantime."

"Ladies, please. Now Dylan's on his way. I just texted him."

While we waited, I filled them in on what had transpired since Belle found Carole Craddock in the Studebaker's home. "How did y'all find out about the cookies and the note?"

Old Man Goodson smiled. "Nothing's a secret in town, you know that, Lilybit."

"Some things are secrets," I said.

The slight nod of his head told me he knew exactly what I was talking about, and it was a secret that would stay between us forever.

"Sounds like that Dabney Coleman gone and killed her bestie," Bonnie said.

"It ain't Dabney Coleman, it's Dabney something else," Millie said.

Clayton," I said.

"Yeah, Clayton. Coleman's the actor you're talking about. The one in the *On Golden Pond* and that movie with Dolly Parton. Think he's been dead for years."

"He ain't dead," Billy Ray said. "Least I don't think so."

"You keep up with the celebrity gossip," Old Man Goodson asked, a touch of humor in his tone.

"I got me a few actors I like. Just watched him in *9 to 5* on cable last week."

"Don't mean he's still alive if they're still showing his movies on the TV," Old Man Goodson said.

"Man's got a lot of time on his hands, and he ain't the sharpest tack in the box," Millie said. She walked back to the counter to help a customer that had just walked in.

"I think Bonnie's right," Old Man Goodson said. He pointed to the note on the table. "Sounds like that Clayton girl had a bone to pick with her partner, and now she's got one to pick with you, too."

Dylan and Matthew came through the door and greeted us all with a head nod. They removed their hats.

My fiancé kissed the top of my head. "Where's the note?"

I pointed to the middle of the table.

The two men read it and then Matthew picked it up with a napkin.

"My fingerprints are on it," I said.

"I figured."

Dylan took the note from Matthew and examined it closely. "Looks like the same font from the other one, but I'd have to have my techs check it to be sure."

"Why don't you got your people protecting our girls?" Billy Ray asked.

Dylan sighed. "If I had my way, they would be, but the county commissioners are tightening their leashes on several county departments. We're over budget on overtime, and they don't think protecting a citizen that–" He narrowed his eyes straight at me. "–sticks her nose where it doesn't belong is a justifiable reason for overtime hours."

I raised an eyebrow, and Dylan held his hands up. "Not my words."

"Good thing we've got a plan then," Bonnie said. She held up her plastic bat.

Matthew chuckled.

"Check out what the boys have," I said.

The two men held up their golf clubs and both Matthew and Dylan nodded.

"Not too shabby," Dylan said.

"Is that a Rogue X?" Matthew asked Billy Ray.

"Don't know. Got it at the Goodwill."

Matthew shook his head. "Definitely no then. Those things run around a hundred bucks, but they're the best out there."

"Our protectors are on a limited budget, too," I said.

"Amen," Old Man Goodson said.

"Y'all aren't really planning on using those things, are you?" I asked.

"Sure are," Bonnie said.

"We're planting our butts right outside your office. That's why Millie here filled that jug with sweet tea. It's goin' to be hard work keeping you and Belle safe."

"You should have worn something a little lighter then," I said.

"The four of you don't need to be—"

I stopped Dylan. "Don't even bother. You know they're going to do what they're going to do regardless of what we say."

"Sounds familiar."

"Funny, I was thinking the same thing."

"I'm the sheriff. They ought to listen to what I say."

"And you should be the one looking out for our girls, but since you're not, someone's got to. Seems we're qualified to do the job," Billy Ray said. He held up his golf club again, and it wobbled back and forth in his hand.

I pressed my lips together, but Matthew couldn't hold back his laughter.

CHAPTER ELEVEN

At the request of the county commissioners, Dylan scheduled a town meeting to update everyone on the investigation. They believed it was good media fodder for the Atlanta news stations, though Dylan wasn't sure any of them would even show up. Nonetheless, he and Matthew headed back to the sheriff's office to prepare for it later that day, and the rest of us walked the few steps to Bramblett County Realty to get to work.

Back at the office, the men sat outside in lawn chairs Old Man Goodson had thrown in the back of his pickup truck, while Henrietta and Bonnie stayed inside, guarding me up close and personal, as Bonnie said.

Belle arrived shortly after they'd settled into their designated spots, and stood outside chatting with the men, an amused smile stretched across her face. She came in giggling. "I just love those two."

Henrietta swung her plastic bat in the air. "Don't you be horning in on our territory or I'm going to have to teach you a thing or two."

"Oh honey, you could teach me a lot of things, I'm sure. But don't worry, I am not horning in on your men. They are just too much for me to handle."

"Sounds about right," Bonnie said.

Belle and I had a quick conversation about the added security, the county commissioners limiting the department's overtime hours, and Billy Ray's increased shaking.

"We ought to get him to a doctor," Belle whispered.

"I was thinking the same thing."

"He won't go to no doctor," Henrietta said.

"We've been telling him for the past month he's got to, but he flat out refuses," Bonnie said.

Henrietta shook her head. "Stubborn old coot."

"But he's our stubborn old coot," Bonnie said. She dug into her large bright orange beach bag. "Speaking of old. I got something for the wedding." She took out a small gift box wrapped in yellow and red balloon gift wrap with happy birthday printed all over it. "Sorry about the paper, but most of my friends are dead, not getting married. Last time I used this was 2002."

Belle practically spit out the sweet tea she'd just sipped.

"Oh, Bonnie, you shouldn't have." I gently tore the wrapping off the box and smiled as I opened it. Inside was a blue lace garter with an intricate pearl floral design. I carefully removed it from the box and gasped. "This is beautiful. Was it yours?"

She nodded. "Didn't have no wedding to speak of, but my momma wanted to make sure I had something special that day, so she made it herself. Wore it under my blue dress on account of we didn't have the money for a real wedding dress, but I didn't mind none. It was the only pretty thing I had for years."

"Why didn't you give this to one of your kids?"

She grunted. "Would have if they'd given me the chance, but neither of them told me they were getting married till after the fact." She pointed to the garter. "Now you got yourself something old. And you know what? Gave myself to my husband for the first time wearing that thing." She laughed. "Had I known what I was getting myself into, I wouldn't have bothered with the darn thing."

"The garter?" I asked.

"Heck no, the marriage."

That time Belle did spit out her sweet tea. I laughed, too.

"Don't get me wrong. I had a long marriage, and most of the time I was happy, but raising a husband and kids takes its toll on a woman. I used to be near five feet six inches, now look at me."

Bonnie wasn't much taller than a bar height counter, and I didn't recall her ever being much taller than that. "You look like a beautiful woman."

"I'm rode hard and put away wet, but I earned these battle scars." She pulled up her sweatshirt. "See this? I used to have me a strong gut, hard as steel I tell ya, and then them two babies dropped out and it all went south."

"Gravity has its effect on everything. But that doesn't matter. It's what's inside that counts."

"What's inside is a whole lotta gas," she said. "I had me two hot dogs last night."

"Ain't nobody need to be around that woman the day after two hotdogs," Henrietta said.

I laughed.

"Oh, and I got something for you, too," Henrietta said. She removed a small box from her bag. "I did have me a wedding dress, one my momma made, and this here matched it perfect."

Her box was wrapped in the same paper as Bonnie's. I opened it and gasped when I saw the beautiful pearl necklace. "This is gorgeous, Henrietta."

Belle leaned in and gasped too.

"Are they real?" I asked. I stole a look at Belle, and I knew she'd mentioned to them that I hadn't found a necklace.

Henrietta shrugged. "Beats me. They were my momma's and her momma's. Just thought they were pretty, never cared what they were made of."

"I don't care either," I said. I hugged both of the women as tears welled up in my eyes. "I love you two so much. Thank you for this. I wish you could come to the wedding."

Henrietta coughed, and Bonnie elbowed her.

What?" I asked.

The men walked in escorting John Rockwell, who carried a large bouquet of red roses. Belle's smile dropped.

"Hey ladies, how y'all doing?" John asked.

"Man here says he's got a special delivery for our Belle, and he refused to leave it with us."

We'd been so caught up in the moment, none of us had noticed them outside.

"It's okay. This is John Rockwell, a fellow realtor," Belle said.

John handed her the bouquet. "For you, my dear."

Belle flinched. "John, that's very kind of you, but you—"

He nodded. "I know, I know. I shouldn't have, but how else am I going to convince you to go out with me?"

"Belle can't go out with you. She's got a man already," Bonnie said.

"And he's a lot better looking than you," Henrietta added.

John Rockwell smirked as he gazed up and down Belle's body. "I don't see a ring on her finger."

Belle glanced at all of us standing there, staring at her. "Can y'all give us a moment, please?"

I scooted everyone back outside while Belle set John Rockwell straight.

A few minutes later, they hugged, which set the men ready to battle, their grips tightening on their golf clubs, but John left with a mere nod to all of us, and not a word.

Belle motioned us back inside.

"What'd you say to him?" Bonnie asked.

"I explained that I'm seriously involved with someone, and that while I appreciate the flowers, I'm simply not interested."

"Good for you," Henrietta said.

"Unfortunately, now I can't pump him for information."

"We should chase him down and make sure he got the message," Billy Ray said.

"That's sweet of you, but it's okay. I think he understands now. I don't think we'll be seeing Mr. Rockwell again any time soon."

While Belle got busy doing what needed to be done to clear our business to-do list before the wedding, I did research on the agents at Craddock & Clayton. Someone left those notes, and it wasn't Dabney Clayton. At least not the first one. She couldn't have left it on my car when she was with me the entire time.

Best case scenario was someone from her firm snuck out and left it while I talked with Dabney. Worst case was someone from outside the firm left it. I decided to start with the best case first.

I scrolled through the agents until I found the few that had been there earlier. The one in the cute dress stood out, and I couldn't help but wonder if she was the one that texted me before. I couldn't say for sure, but if I went with my gut like Dylan said, I'd have said yes, it was her. The way she couldn't look me in the eye, something about it convinced me it was her.

I unplugged my laptop and walked it over to Belle at our conference table. "Hey, can you help me with something?"

Bonnie and Henrietta perked up from snoozing across from Belle.

"What's going on?" Bonnie asked.

I waved them off. "Nothing. Just need my partner's help. Go back to sleep."

Henrietta was already snoring again.

"What's up?" Belle asked.

I explained what I needed, and she picked up the phone and made the call. "Yes, hi. I'm interested in a home you've got listed."

After going through a fairly strong pre-qualifying lie that included a great grandmother of the Dunwoody Sanders family recently dying and leaving her a bunch of money, Belle—and I—had an appointment to see a property listed by Craddock & Clayton's Kizzie Warbly.

"Let's go," I said.

Belle pointed to the snoring duo at the conference table. "What about them?"

I quietly gathered my things. "If we can make it past them, we can make it past the dueling freight trains outside."

Belle glanced at Old Man Goodson and Billy Ray, who were heads back and mouths open in the lawn chairs outside. "Bless their hearts, they really tried."

I smiled. "A security person's job is never done."

We snuck out without jarring any of them from sweet slumber and promised to needle them about it upon our return.

The home wasn't far from Bramblett, and while we drove, I mapped out what we needed to accomplish.

"How about we just cut to the chase and ask her what she knows?"

"That could work too," I said.

Kizzie Warbly was already inside when we arrived. And if I said she wasn't thrilled to see me, that wouldn't quite express her true sentiment. When she saw me, she grabbed her purse off the kitchen counter and hightailed it toward the front door. Belle, however, wasn't having any of it and blocked her. I came up behind her and covered a sneak out the back.

"I should have known something was up with that call. I've never heard of any Dunwoody Sanders family."

"Cash sales are like dangling a carrot in front of a horse, aren't they?" Belle asked.

"What do you want?"

I asked her to sit and was surprised when she did.

"We want to know what happened to Carole Craddock," I said. "And I think you may know something."

She rubbed her hands together as her eyes darted back and forth between Belle and me. "I don't know anything."

"You're the one that texted me, aren't you?"

Her eyes widened and she hesitated before shaking her head. "No, I didn't."

"Kizzie," I leaned forward and softened my voice. "I promise you I won't let Dabney know what you tell us, but I know you know something. I saw the way you were looking at me earlier. Did you leave the note on my car?"

"Note? What note?"

That wasn't the reaction I'd expected. "You didn't leave a note on my car earlier today?"

She leaned her head back and sighed as she pressed her palms into her thighs. "I was the one that texted you, but I swear, I didn't leave a note on your car. What did it say?"

"Basically, that I needed to keep my nose out of the situation."

"That's good advice."

"Why did you tell me Dabney isn't innocent? Do you think she killed Carole?"

"No, I mean, yes. I...I'm not sure, but I think she and Floyd are involved."

"What makes you think that?"

She shifted in her seat. "Last week Floyd came to the office, and I heard him and Carole arguing. I couldn't make out the entire conversation, but from what I heard, Carole was upset with Floyd about some sales he'd taken from her."

"Did she say how he was doing it?"

"She accused Dabney of giving him a list of homes Carole was close to making offers on. Said he did what he'd always done and went in making offers before she could."

"Dabney's undercutting her own business? That doesn't make sense," Belle said.

"It does if she's planning to partner with Floyd, and that's the talk in the office. I think she wanted to stop Carole from taking the business to Rockwell, so she set up the thing with Floyd because she knew he'd do it." She curled her upper lip. "Didn't take much to convince him. From what I've heard, she just had to get a little personal, if you know what I mean."

Belle grimaced. "Ew."

"You're telling me. That man is disgusting."

"Everyone has their own tastes." I crossed my legs and set out asking her a small list of questions. "Why do you think Carole decided to leave the partnership and work with Skip?"

"I don't know, but what I've heard is that she was going in to modernize the firm. Skip's old school, and even though Carole's not young, she's hip to social media marketing, and she knows how to talk to millennials. She could really bring a modern feel to his firm. I was considering moving over there. I just wanted to wait until she'd settled in before saying anything. You know, in case it didn't pan out or something."

"Which is didn't," Belle said.

"No, it didn't."

"Is there a way to verify that Dabney and Floyd were doing what you say?"

She shrugged. "Other than my seeing her give him copies of client files, no. But I'm not sure I'm the only one that saw that happen. We have several agents who could have seen it happening another time, but I'd have no way of knowing."

"Do you think Dabney is planning to merge the firm with Floyd's?"

She nodded. "It's a smart move if you ask me. They're both powerhouses, and if they were doing it to stop Carole, it would have worked."

"You think Carole was a better agent?"

She laughed. "I don't think it, I know it. She had every award from local to national ones, and trust me, she made sure people knew. If you look at her personal page on the website, she's got them all listed. She was much better at closing than Dabney is."

"So, you think Dabney and Floyd killed Carole because she's a better realtor than them?"

"It's the only plausible reason. Sure, most agents in town despised the woman. She wasn't easy to work for, that's for sure, but even those that didn't work for her didn't like her. She wasn't a bad person, she was just a good salesperson, and people were jealous."

Jealousy. I'd have to add that to the list of reasons people killed.

Passion, territory, money, betrayal, and jealousy.

Carole could have been murdered by anyone that felt inferior, that was threatened by her success, but I didn't think that was the case. When I factored in the client stealing, the partner switching, the creepy relationship between Floyd Bowman and Dabney Clayton, I couldn't step away mentally from their probable guilt. It just fit.

"I noticed the coffee station in your office. Are there always cookies on it?"

She nodded. "All the time. Carole is—was— a cookie addict. That woman had a cookie in her hand almost all the time. Everyone knew if they wanted to be on her good side, they needed to bring her cookies."

Everyone? Great. That just made the suspect list a mile long.

We thanked Kizzie and swore we'd keep her name out of things if we could but said we wouldn't hide anything from the police if asked.

CHAPTER TWELVE

Dylan wore a freshly pressed uniform and adjusted the microphone on the podium in front of him. It was a beautiful, if not toasty, late afternoon in Bramblett, and the town square was the perfect spot for the town meeting.

Only we weren't doing it in the right spot of the town square. Instead of standing out of the obnoxious heat near the small covered grandstand, we stood outside his office which faced the setting sun bouncing off the building and onto everyone who'd come out for the meeting.

It was hotter than blazes, as my momma always said. I waved my hand toward my face. "Whoo, it's egg frying hot."

"You think that waving is going to help?" Belle asked. She stuck her hand in her bag and pulled out a little battery-operated fan. She clicked it on, and it hummed as it blew air on her face.

"Jealous," I said.

She removed another one from her purse. "I thought you'd think that."

"Oh, thank you. You're so sweet."

"That's what I like people to think."

Dylan tapped on the mic. "Afternoon everyone. How about we get this started? I'm sure everyone wants to get home to their air conditioning and a good dinner."

"Is he kidding? This town lives for this stuff," Belle said.

"He knows that. He's just hoping they'll leave right when he's done. He hates these things."

"As you all know, an out of town realtor was found dead in a local resident's home, and we've been actively investigating the case," Dylan said.

Three networks had shown up to video the meeting, but Dylan wasn't nervous. "Carole

Craddock died from a slow acting poison called sulfate dioxin. In liquid form, sulfate dioxin has no smell or taste, and it typically takes about five hours for symptoms to appear. Unfortunately, at that time, it's too late. Rapid heartbeat, headache, dizziness, and sweating occur, ultimately ending in cardiac arrest, as was the case with Ms. Craddock. The problem with that is these are common symptoms for a long list of ailments, and by the time a person realizes it might be serious, as I said, it's too late."

A media person raised his hand but spoke before Dylan gave him the go ahead. "Was the poison found in the cookies?"

"There is no evidence to suggest the cookie in Ms. Craddock's stomach caused her death."

Belle nudged my arm. "What? Is that true?"

"This is the first I'm hearing of it."

The crowd gasped. Word had gotten around about the cookies, and to hear they weren't the cause of her death shocked the town.

"Did she inhale it? Was it rubbed onto her skin?"

"Sulfate dioxin is a powered substance, easily dissolved, but it's not something that someone typically applies to the skin or inhales."

"So, you can't say for sure if one of those didn't happen?"

"No, I can't say for sure."

"Do you have any suspects?"

"We are actively working the investigation and expect to have it closed within a matter of days."

"Who is your number one suspect? Are you planning to make any arrests?"

"We've asked several people in for further questioning."

"Can we get their names?"

"We're keeping the persons of interest confidential at this time."

"Did you know they had persons of interest?" Belle asked.

"I assumed, but Dylan's not saying a lot about it."

"When do you expect to make an arrest?" The same reporter asked.

"As I said, we expect to have this investigation closed in a few days."

"We should have this wrapped up within twenty-four hours," one of the county commissioners said.

Dylan's face remained stoic, but I know that frustrated him. He didn't like anyone speaking for him, regardless of their political position.

Belle nudged my arm. "Look who's here." She pointed in front of us.

Skip and John Rockwell moved up in the crowd, only a few feet away from us.

"Interesting," I said.

Bonnie and Henrietta pushed their way through the mass of people and settled in behind the Rockwell men.

"And that's how you snoop," Belle said.

I smiled. "They're the masters of it, aren't they?"

Henrietta flipped around, caught us staring at them and gave us a thumbs up.

I checked out the rest of the crowd and found both Floyd Bowman and Dabney Clayton on opposite ends of the group, of course.

"Lots of interesting people here for this, don't you think?" Belle asked.

"Emm hmm. I'm sure they're the people Dylan was talking about when he said they're bringing in people for further questioning." I glanced at the Rockwell men and then at Floyd and Dabney. "The super couple is keeping their distance from each other though. Isn't that interesting?"

"Probably don't want to seem suspicious."

"Yes, but they don't know what we know."

"Bless their hearts, they think we're the small-town folk without brains, don't they?"

"Sure seems like it."

"As I said, we're actively working the investigation, and are doing our best to close the case as quickly as possible." He adjusted the microphone. "What we need from all of you is for you to go on with your daily activities as usual. We do not believe the murderer is a threat to anyone else in town."

"But can you be sure?" A resident asked.

"We can assure you we're doing everything within our power to keep the community safe."

"I don't see no extra deputies on the roads. You gonna bring in some help? I got me a family, and I can't be home keeping them safe 'cause I got to work," another resident said.

"Sir, I assure you we have plenty of deputies to keep your family safe," that same county commissioner said.

I was not his biggest fan.

"But I heard you're cutting budgets, and the sheriff took a big hit. What's that mean for us?" The man asked.

"Yeah, how're they supposed to keep us safe from all these killers coming into our little community?" A man from the back hollered.

"Budget cuts do not impact the safety of our community," the county commissioner said. "And I assure you, you are safe to go about your usual activities. The woman murdered wasn't a local resident. She just happened to be here when she took her last breath."

"I do not like that man," Belle said.

"Hopefully we'll get to vote him out in the next election."

"Honey, that man ain't gonna make it to the next election. The town'll push him out if he keeps that know it all attitude he's got."

"Let's hope they do it legally."

"This is North Georgia. We do what needs to be done up here."

"That's what I'm afraid of."

She smiled. "Me, too."

We waited around for Dylan as the crowd faded to only a few stragglers. They'd brought their popcorn and lawn chairs and drank their moonshine out of a thermos like no one had a clue what they were doing. The thing was, everyone knew what was in those thermoses, they just didn't care.

Some battles were more important than others.

Bonnie and Henrietta rushed over as fast as two women no longer steady on their feet could rush. I loved those two and I worried for their old bodies. Young at heart only went so far.

"We got our killer," Bonnie said.

"And we think they're planning another one," Henrietta said.

"What are you talking about?" Belle asked.

"That boy that was courting you? Him and that man over there with him, they're up to something."

"They're up to murder, that's what they's up to," Bonnie said.

"What did you hear?" I asked.

"They's up to something, that's for sure. The younger man, the one that brought the flowers, he was telling the other man—"

"The younger man is John Rockwell. The older one is his daddy, Skip," I said.

"That John one, he was telling his pa he's got to get rid of her, that she ain't no good," Bonnie said.

My eyes widened. "Who were they talking about?"

She shrugged.

"But," Henrietta said, "his pa said he was working on it, and he'd have her gone in no time, and he might could hold his horses so he doesn't cause people to wonder what's going on."

"I'll get Matthew," Belle said, and rushed off.

Belle pointed to them as she talked to Matthew. She came back over as he headed toward them.

"They were here at Dylan's request," she said.

"Good. Looks like they got them their killers," Bonnie said.

I caught a glimpse of another deputy guiding Dabney Clayton, who was also being led toward the sheriff's office. "I'm not so sure who the killer is, but it's one of them. I just know it."

Before anyone had a chance to snatch up Floyd too, I bolted to him. I wanted to ask him about his business relationship with Dabney Clayton and get as much out of him as I could.

"How's the merger coming along?"

He shifted his weight to his right leg and attempted to act casual, but his widened eyes gave his nervousness away. "What makes you think I'd go into business with Dabney?"

"I didn't say anything about Dabney."

He grimaced.

"But since you asked, it's the same thing that makes me see why you'd have an intimate relationship with her. Money."

He flinched. "I'm not sure what you're talking about."

"I think you are, and here's what else I think. I think it's been you manipulating Carole's sales opportunities to your benefit, not the other way around, like Skip said, and I think Dabney knows that. When Carole decided, for whatever reason, to leave her own firm and work with Skip Rockwell, Dabney came to you, told you what homes Carole's clients would be making offers on, because we both know as owners of their agency, they'd share that information, and then you'd go in and get one of your clients to make an offer first."

He sighed. "It's not what you think."

"So, you're saying I'm wrong?"

"Yes. No. Yes, I mean, you're right, Dabney was feeding me information about Carole's offers, and yes, I did go in and take one or two of them, but not because I'm going into business with Dabney."

"Then what is it?"

He hesitated, dragging his hand down his cheeks and chin and then rubbing his neck.

"Carole screwed me over one too many times, so when Dabney gave me the opportunity to stick it to her, I took it. It's as simple as that."

"Why exactly would Dabney give you that opportunity? What was in it for her?"

"You heard the rumors. She thought Carole was going to work with Skip."

"Thought and knew are two different things. She could have just asked her."

"She knew something was going on, we just weren't sure what."

"We?"

He smiled. "Me and Dabney. We're in love."

"Anyone will tell you love is a motive for murder." I stared at the ground for a moment and then back up at Floyd Bowman. "And you'd know Carole loved cookies because Dabney could have told you."

"The sheriff said the cookies didn't kill her." He laughed. "And even if they did, you think that'd be my weapon of choice? You're crazy. I'm a horrible cook, and my baking skills are even worse. You can ask Dabney. I even took a class to try and improve, but I burned the cookies. That's how bad I cook." He sighed again. "Listen, I didn't like Carole. I admit that, and yeah, I was taking sales out from under her, but I didn't kill her."

CHAPTER THIRTEEN

I snuggled with Bo on my couch while Dylan stretched his legs out and rested them on my coffee table. I wanted to ask him about the cookies right away, and normally, I would, but I also wanted to ask him if he'd made an arrest. He wasn't exactly forthcoming with information as he yawned and closed his eyes. "Did you make an arrest?"

He smiled at me and then leaned his head back again. "Nope. Everything we've got is circumstantial." He shifted his head and sighed my direction. "Would you believe the three of them accused each other?"

"But what about what Bonnie and Henrietta heard?"

"There's an agent Belle's suitor wants fired. He's putting pressure on his dad to do it."

"Oh."

He laughed. "I appreciate their effort, but those two don't know how to solve a murder. Investigator kits and all."

"Don't forget the plastic baseball bats."

"How could I?"

"Is the commissioner right? Are you going to make an arrest soon?"

"Not with what we've got so far."

I nestled in close. "I had a talk with one of the agents from Carole's firm, and she said Carole loved cookies. She also said if someone wanted on her good side, all they had to do was bring in cookies. There was a coffee and snack station in the office with a bunch of cookies, and when I first talked to Dabney Clayton, she was eating one."

"Yes, we've seen the cookies."

"You said the cookies weren't what killed Carole. Is that true?"

"I said the cookies found in her stomach weren't the cause of her death."

"I don't understand."

"There was traces of the poison in her stomach as well as remains of what the lab tested as chocolate chip cookies and sulfate dioxide in her intestines and colon."

"But you said—"

"There are some parts of the investigation we don't make public and that's one of them. If the killer thinks we're clueless, he'll get lazy. Lazy killers are easy to catch."

"Or her."

"Or her."

"So, what you're saying is the cookies at the Studebaker's home aren't the ones that killed her?"

He nodded once.

"But she'd eaten a cookie or cookies possibly, that had poisoning in it?"

He nodded again.

"Which could have come from anywhere."

"Unfortunately, yes, but we have a few leads."

"Care to share them?"

"I do not."

I groaned. "Fine. I'm sure I'll figure it out eventually."

"I don't doubt that one bit." His upper lip twitched. "I'm looking forward to it, actually."

"What happened with Skip and John Rockwell? The way Bonnie said it, their conversation sounded ominous."

"To her, I'm sure it did, but they verified, separately, they were discussing a woman in their firm. One they wanted to fire, not murder."

"Poor Bonnie. Bless her heart. She tried."

"She sure did."

I reiterated what Kizzie Warbly told us earlier.

"Can she prove Dabney gave any files to Floyd?"

"I'm not sure. Would you like me to find out?"

He shook his head. "How about you let the sheriff handle that?"

"I might could do that. I've heard he's not too bad at doing his job."

Dylan laughed. "If you'd give him a chance to do it, he might actually solve a case or two."

It was my turn to laugh. "If you'd do it faster, there wouldn't be an issue."

"Ouch."

"Kizzie was pretty adamant that Dabney didn't want Skip and Carole taking her business. She thinks that's why she gave it to

Floyd. He'd have to split it with her though, or else, what's the point?"

"If they were planning to merge firms, it would all make sense. Get the business before Carole can."

"And when that started to fall apart, they killed Carole. That way, the business would stay with Dabney, and she could just transfer it to the other firm." It made sense, but I knew something was off. I just wasn't quite sure what. "But wait. That doesn't make sense."

"Why not?"

"First of all, Floyd told me they weren't merging firms. He said they were in love."

"He told us that, too, but that doesn't mean it's the truth."

"But with Carole dead, what purpose does Floyd serve Dabney if they aren't really in love? Why would Dabney need to merge the firms then? Why wouldn't she just continue on her own without a partner at all? And why would she continue the ruse with Floyd if she doesn't love him?"

Dylan considered my question, but before he had a chance to speak, I blurted out, "Maybe because Dabney can't effectively manage the business. Maybe that's what

Carole did, and with her dead, Dabney needs Floyd?"

"We're already working that angle."

"I think that's the route to take. I feel like Dabney's not being genuine, and maybe poor Floyd is being screwed over. And besides, he said he can't cook. He even said he took a cooking class and burned the cookies."

He laughed. "I can't relate to burned cookies. Never happens to me."

"And you've actually baked cookies how many times exactly?"

His lip curled. "Two."

"Huh. I've had them both times then?"

He nodded. "Because I baked them for you."

I smiled. "That's sweet, but how 'bout you stick to the grill from now on?"

"After the wedding, I'm going to bake you up the biggest, best batch of chocolate chip cookies you've ever had, just to prove my point."

My mood changed. "Dylan, I'm worried. We don't have much time. The wedding is close. What happens if you don't make an arrest before we have to leave? You and Matthew both can't run off to Italy in the middle of an investigation, and with the way the county commissioners have been acting, I don't think they'd let you if you tried."

He held my hand. "Honey, we're going to Italy, and this case is going to be solved before then, I promise."

I nuzzled into him. "You can't promise that."

"I can promise to do everything possible to make that happen. How's that?"

"Better than nothing, I suppose."

He sighed. "We'll solve Carole Craddock's murder, Lily Bean. And we'll do it before we have to leave for Italy."

CHAPTER FOURTEEN

Our highly trained and physically fit security guards were ready and waiting for us when Belle and I arrived for a quick breakfast at Millie's Café, their plastic bats and golf clubs in hand.

Thankfully they'd chosen to dress in clothing more weather appropriate. "I love your dress," I told Bonnie. "The yellow is stunning."

"Oh, thank you. I got me this at the Goodwill day before the boys got them clubs. It's a little big, but I'll stitch it up when we're done solving this murder."

"Well, I think it's perfect."

Bonnie and Henrietta had adorable taste in clothing. Their potato sack style dresses, something like a house dress I assumed, always included bright colors and large prints, and jelly shoes that perfectly matched the dresses dominant color.

"What's for breakfast," Belle asked.

"Biscuits with a side of white gravy and grits," Billy Ray said. He stuffed a big bite into his mouth and moaned. "Best gravy in the South if you ask me."

"Not going to argue that," Belle said. She stuck her finger in the gravy, scooped up a bit onto it, and licked it clean. "Yum." She hollered over to Millie for her own serving.

We tried to convince the crew we didn't need security, but they wouldn't hear it. They insisted on doing their part so the wedding could would happen.

"We don't want our Lilybit to be a spinster any longer."

"Hey, what about me?" Belle asked.

Bonnie shrugged. "Pigs'll fly before you finally settle down."

"Bless your heart. Maybe one day that Matthew will decide you're a keeper," Henrietta said.

I drummed my fingers on the table and looked away so I wouldn't laugh.

The mood shifted when Dabney Clayton walked into Millie's, her head held high, and an air of snobbiness coming off of her in waves.

"Well, well, I knew I'd find you here. You small-town realtors don't work all that hard now, do you?"

Belle rolled her eyes. "We just work smarter than you uppity city folk, that's all.

Dabney glanced at her watch. "It's almost nine o'clock. Shouldn't your office be open by now? I've been knocking on that door for a good ten minutes."

"What do you need, Ms. Clayton?" I asked.

"I need you to mind your own business, that's what I need." She stood over me. "I know you're telling that sheriff of yours lies, and I'm telling you to stop before I get my attorney involved."

"Might could do you some good to get that attorney involved right quick anyway," Old Man Goodson said. "Looks like you're going to be headed to the slammer soon."

My eyes darted to my older friend and I hoped he knew I wanted him to hush.

"I didn't kill Carole. She wasn't worth my time, so why would I risk my freedom with such a waste of a person?"

"Because she was leaving your firm to work with someone else," I said.

"I was done with her anyway."

"Then how about because she planned to take clients with her? Clients you wanted to keep at your firm."

"You don't know what you're talking about, but if you keep saying things and keep bothering my agents, I'm going to have you arrested for harassment."

Bonnie had had enough. She pushed herself up from her chair and stood up to Dabney. The top of her head reached just below Dabney's chin, so she backed away a bit and glared up at the woman. "You got no right coming in here and threatening our Lilybit, you hear me? This is our town, and we don't behave like that here. You want to act like you don't stink to high heaven, that your soul ain't blacker than the night, that's fine. Just do that in your own neck of the woods. We don't want your kind here."

Dabney's jaw dropped, but she quickly recovered, swapping the shocked expression for a snotty smile. "Well, aren't you just adorable, acting all big, and tall, and strong, and brave." She tapped Bonnie on the head with her finger. "When I could tip you over with one finger."

Millie stood next to Dabney and tapped on her shoulder. Millie wasn't tall, but she was broad, and I suspected she could still hold her own in an old-time saloon if need be. "It's time you get on out of my café before I throw you out on that skinny little butt of yours, you hear? I don't need to call the sheriff. I'll take care of you myself."

Dabney flinched and then pointed at me. "Stay out of my way, Miss Sprayberry."

As she turned around and began to walk away, Henrietta stuck out her plastic bat, and since Dabney's nose so far up in the air, she didn't see it and went sailing onto the ground, nose first. She yelped as her face hit her arm, which thankfully for her, she'd flung out to stop the fall.

We all just sat there, staring as she rushed to get up, wiped off her outfit, and scooted out with her tail between her legs. When the café door closed behind her, Bonnie, Henrietta, Millie and the men hooted and hollered, as did the rest of the people in the café. Belle and I stared at each other, both of us forcing straight, serious faces, but not for long.

We couldn't contain our laughter either.

"Goodness Henrietta, remind me not to mess with you," Belle said.

"Darn straight," Bonnie said.

"That's what happens when someone threatens the people we love," Henrietta said.

* * *

"I really hope we're like those two when we're their age," Belle said. She'd just finished the last of the filing she'd promised she'd finish before the wedding. She dropped into her office chair. "I'm glad you talked them out of hanging out in here. I love them, but there's a lot to do before we leave, and they can be a bit distracting."

"That snoring, for sure."

"Oh my gosh, can you believe it? They're louder than Bo."

"They'd scare Bo awake with that noise. And I wouldn't say I talked them out of it. I'd call it insisted."

"Strongly insisted."

"With a bribe."

"Hey, if offering to pay for them to all have a fancy dinner in Alpharetta is a bribe, it's worth it. Besides, just seeing them get all gussied up and go out on the town will be worth it."

"We won't actually see it, Belle. We'll be in Italy, but either way, I'm glad they're not as interested in worrying about me as they are interested in a chunk of red meat and a baked potato."

She laughed. "I can't wait for Italy. If Matthew and I get married, we're having a destination wedding, too. I'm thinking Santorini. Those white buildings with the blue on them? I've seen so many photos of brides there, it's just gorgeous."

I spun my chair toward hers. "Do you think you two will get married?"

She shrugged. "I don't think I'd say no if he asked."

"Oh my gosh, that's huge Belle, huge!"

She waved her hand at me. "The man's got to ask first."

"He'll ask. How could he not? You're amazing."

"Ah, well, yes, that is true."

I threw a pencil at her. "And modest."

"Of course."

My cell phone rang, and when I checked it and saw it was my momma, I dreaded answering it, something I never felt when she called. I didn't want her to think the wedding might not happen, but Bramblett being Bramblett, I suspected someone had filled her in on what was going on, and she was worried. Momma always worried.

"Hey Momma. I was just thinking about you."

"Sweetie, what's going on? I hear you found another dead body? You have got to stop putting yourself in harm's way like that. What'll we do if something happens to you? Your daddy and I are getting all set for the wedding, but I heard you may have to cancel now because of that dead person?"

"Momma, first of all, I didn't find the body, Belle did, and no, as of now, the wedding is not being canceled. Actually, it wouldn't be canceled at all. Maybe postponed, but Dylan promised me that won't happen, and I'm not all that worried."

"Now don't you lie to me. They can't solve a murder when they don't even have a suspect. What's your fiancé doing not having a suspect?"

Sometimes the gossip reached farther than necessary, and when it did, it wasn't at all like the truth. "He's doing his job, Momma." The woman was sweeter than Millie's tea, but when someone pressed her panic button, there was no stopping the worry. I gave it my best shot though. "My dress is being sent over there as we speak, and Belle and I were just sitting here talking about what we have left to do before we leave. It's all fine, I promise." I hoped that was true.

"I sure hope so. Your daddy can't make that long flight without taking something to calm his nerves, and you know how he hates taking pills. Can barely swallow them now since he's quit smoking."

I wasn't sure how the two were related, but I didn't dare ask, either. "I promise, if Dylan thinks we can't make it, I'll let you know right away, okay?"

"You think that's going to happen? I sure hope it ain't."

"I don't think so."

We chatted a little longer, her blurting out her concern about a canceled wedding and what that would mean for my future, and while I normally would have been concerned about a canceled wedding, her panic made me see the hyperbole of it all and eased my nerves. I knew that no matter what, Dylan and I would get married, even if it meant we did it at the county courthouse in front of a judge. I'd stopped caring about the wedding itself and cared more about the actual marriage. Being Mrs. Lily Roberts for the rest of my life was more important than the event itself. We hung up with her feeling an ounce better about my pending nuptials.

Belle moaned. "I didn't even talk to her, and I'm exhausted."

"She's just being Momma."

"Who do you think told her?"

"You know how it works. I'm sure half the town called her. She gets calls all the time about what her daughter's up to. Sometimes I think I should have left town like my brothers did. She doesn't know anyone where they live."

She laughed. "You'll never leave here. You're too attached to these nosy people."

"I know. It's a love hate relationship sometimes, but it's charming in its own way. After the fact maybe, but when you're in the heat of the gossip, it's exhausting."

She raised her eyebrow. "You haven't thought about leaving, have you?"

"Dylan's an elected official. If he's not re-elected again, it's possible we'll have to leave."

She shrugged. "I'm not worried about that. He'll be re-elected every time he runs. He's a great sheriff."

"What about you and Matthew? Is he going to be content as a deputy sheriff indefinitely?"

"He's said for the time being, that's perfect, but he's got some embers in the fire for another business, and I think, if that happens, he'll do both until he can get the other one up and running successfully."

"Another business?"

She held her finger to her lips. "I'm not supposed to say anything yet."

"Got it. Then I won't press."

"Thank you. You know I'd tell you if you did."

"I know, and that's why I'm not pushing the issue. So, you'd better let it go, too."

"Fine." She covered her mouth with her hand. "I'll do my best," she mumbled.

The mail came, and Belle tossed me three bills, two finalized contracts an agent refused to scan to us, and an information flyer about a realtor open house the following week.

I threw the flyer into the garbage. "Won't be going to that."

"There goes free snacks, right down the drain," she said.

"Hopefully the food in Italy is better than those roll up wraps from Costco."

"I have a feeling it is." I finished up some work, responding to emails from other agents and marketing firms we'd never use, and then asked if Belle wanted to come with me to my last showing before the big day.

"I'd love to, but I can't. I'm almost caught up here, and I'm on a roll. Plus, Matthew said he might come by if he gets a break, and we might grab a late lunch at Millie's or get a slice of pizza."

"No worries. I'll be back soon." I headed out the door, saying goodbye to Old Man Goodson and Billy Ray on my way out.

* * *

I didn't make it back to the main strip in town until just before six, when I had to pick up Bo at daycare. When I pulled back up in front of the office, I recognized the car parked in the next space immediately.

I walked around to Bo's side of the car and let him out. "Bo, be nice." He ran up to the office entrance. "And by nice, I mean jump on him and ruin those fancy pants he's wearing."

John Rockwell flinched and backed up into the conference table when Bo bounded into our office heading straight toward him. He stood near John and barked. Belle and I shared a look. As close as we were, I couldn't read her mind, but sometimes I wished I could. That was one of those times. Bo's mind, I could read. If he didn't like someone, they knew. He barked at them and stood near them, almost acting as a shield between the person and his person.

I loved that about my mutt.

John Rockwell pushed further into the table and finally scooted toward the other side. In his defense, Bo was part Boxer, but also part Pit Bull, and the muscled brownish beige mass topped onto long legs with big mouth was intimidating.

"Back dog," he said, his voice an octave higher than usual.

"Bo, sit."

Bo sat, but he still kept his big mouth up close and personal so John Rockwell couldn't or wouldn't, make a move.

"What brings you to town?" I asked. I kept my eye on Belle.

"Oh, John's just come by to check on me, that's all." Her sweet voice was a sign of tolerance and caution on her part. I took note.

"Didn't Belle's talk sink in? She's got a boyfriend."

He narrowed his eyes at me, and it alarmed me. "It's a free world. I can't be arrested for just checking on a friend now, can I?"

I wouldn't exactly call he and Belle friends.

"I appreciate it, John, really, but I'm fine. We're fine," she said.

"There's a murderer loose in your town, and I know you've got that sheriff boyfriend of yours looking out for you, but I wouldn't feel right if I didn't come by and check on you, too."

"Why? Is there something you know that the police don't?" I asked.

He shifted toward me. "I know murderers on the loose and pretty women don't mix, and I wanted to offer my help in any way I can."

How I wished at that moment that Henrietta was there to trip him with her plastic bat, or that Old Man Goodson or Billy Ray would have stuck around to try with their golf clubs. John Rockwell was slimy, and I didn't like him. I didn't want him hurt but put off balance wouldn't be a bad thing. "Your help isn't needed, Mr. Rockwell."

Belle's eyebrows nearly hit the top of her hair line. "But we appreciate the thought." She pushed me aside and stood closer to him. "It's very nice of you."

"I'd like to have you over for dinner." He was looking at Belle, but he moved to the side and smiled at me. "Both of you."

"Oh, that's so sweet," Belle said.

"I think I'll pass. I've got a wedding to get to soon."

"You won't want to miss my cooking. I consider myself a chef of sorts. I've been cooking for years, and recently dove back into the whole creating a meal from the appetizer to the dessert process. I'd love to have you over to give my creations a try."

"Thanks, but I'm busy," I said.

"Like I said, that's very sweet, but I don't think it's a good idea, John." Belle placed her hand on his shoulder. "I really am happily involved with someone. I appreciate the offer though."

"Isn't Matthew coming by to take you to dinner?" I asked. I knew they'd planned on a lunch, but what John Rockwell didn't know would get him out of my office faster. I hoped.

"Then I'll be going," he said. He smiled at me again, and all I wanted to do was take a shower. "Belle, if you change your mind, you know how to reach me." He headed toward the door with Bo at his heels.

Belle closed and locked the door behind him.

"That man's all hat and no cattle."

Belle laughed. "You have to admit, though, he's got impeccable taste in women."

I rolled my eyes. "He rubs me the wrong way."

"But he cooks."

"So he says."

"True, and he's not really my type anyway. I'm not into the ex-fraternity boy who still wears his polo shirts with the little animal on the chest. Showing designer logos is so retro and not my thing."

I laughed because Belle loved a good designer outfit, and she knew it. She just didn't like John Rockwell. Compared to Matthew there was no comparison.

"I am give slap out," she said. She leaned against her desk and Bo came over and licked her foot. "Thanks for the kisses, sweetie. From the looks of things, you're the only boy that'll have time to kiss me tonight."

"Welcome to my life."

"Matthew said they're close to making an arrest. He thinks we'll have no problem making the wedding."

"Seriously? Dylan hasn't told me that." I leaned against her desk too, but Bo didn't try to lick my foot. "What else did Matthew say?"

"Just that."

"Just that?"

"Yup." She looked away when she said that.

"You're lying." Belle was my best friend. I knew her almost as well as I knew myself, even better sometimes, so it wasn't easy for her to get a lie past me. Her physical cues; not making eye contact, staring at the ground, those were obvious, but the subtle cues, the slight fluctuation in her tone, the barely there hesitation in speaking, those were the tells only people like me saw.

"I am not."

"He didn't tell you who they think killed Carole Craddock?"

She stared straight into my eyes. "No, he didn't tell me who they think killed Carole Craddock."

She told the truth then. She'd fibbed about something before, but I didn't press her. Belle didn't fib with malice intent. She fibbed for other reasons and none of them unethical, manipulative, or deceiving. She did it when she had a plan.

And that was what scared me the most, Belle having a plan. "You're up to something."

"I am not," she fibbed.

"Bless your heart, you think I don't know you better than anyone else. How naïve of you."

"Honey, I am a whole lot of things, but I am not naïve."

I laughed and then poked the bear. "And I'm not a nosy control freak."

She laughed, too. "I'd be lying if I agreed with that."

Whatever she had up her sleeve, I hoped and prayed it wouldn't wind up embarrassing me. She had a knack for doing that intentionally.

CHAPTER FIFTEEN

I tapped on Dylan's opened office door while Bo rushed in without the go ahead. "Got a minute for your fiancée and her ill-mannered mutt?"

He stood, pet the pooch, walked over to me and gave me a tight hug. "I've always got time for you and this little guy." He gave Bo's big old head a scratch.

I closed the door behind us. "Rumor has it you're close to making an arrest in the murder investigation?"

He sat at his desk, and I took the seat on the opposite side.

"I had a feeling you'd find out."

"Why didn't you tell me?"

"I planned to, but close doesn't mean we're there yet, and to be honest, I wanted to see if you drew the same conclusion from your quazi-investigation."

I wasn't sure if I should be insulted by that or not, but I was a little bit. "So, you're saying you wanted to compare my quazi-investigation to your professional one before making an official arrest? Why? Because you think I'm a better investigator?"

Because sometimes I felt that way.

"That's not what I mean, and I'm sorry you took it wrong."

I smiled. "You're forgiven."

"We have the same possible suspects, and I'm curious about what you're probably not telling me, and what that could mean."

"What makes you think I'm not telling you something?"

"The fact that you're breathing."

I laughed. "Honestly, I've told you about everything I know, and if I had to choose a main suspect right now, my gut still thinks it's Dabney Clayton. Is that where you're leaning?"

"What makes you think it's her over the others?"

I counted out my reasons. "One, she was so callous when I first talked to her. She showed complete disregard for the fact that her partner had just died. That's a big red flag. They had to have had some good times together, some type of decent relationship to go into business together in the first place. I expected even a smidgen of sadness from her, but nope. Not a bit. Second, I'm not the most romantically experienced woman out there—"

"I disagree with that."

I smiled. "You aside, but I do think a woman knows when another woman is being an opportunist, and I just can't imagine Dabney choosing to be romantically involved with Floyd Bowman without another reason. Call it that gut you tell me to use, but I don't think I'm wrong."

"I'm with you on that."

"So, you think she did it?"

"I think there's a pull toward her, and we're in the process of getting a warrant to go through her business files and bank accounts."

"So, you think I'm right? That she can't manage the business, and that's why she's going into business with Floyd?"

He nodded. "That's what we're aiming toward. We should have the answers later today. I called in a favor, and the forensic team from Forsyth County has agreed to help my guy go through it all."

"So, you think you'll arrest her?"

"If the hunch I have plays out, yes. But, Lily, I need you to keep this to yourself. And Belle needs to, too. If this gets out, it could ruin the investigation."

"And the wedding."

"And the wedding."

I promised him I'd keep my mouth shut, and since Matthew hadn't given Belle an actual name, I didn't think she'd blab anything either, though I wouldn't expect her to if he had. "Speaking of Belle, do you know what she's hiding? I caught her fibbing earlier, so I know she's up to something."

Dylan smirked and looked away, and I knew he knew, too. "Don't have a clue."

"Emm hmm. Y'all are involved, aren't you? It just better not screw up the wedding."

"It won't, I promise."

I was grateful that he said it with such a guarantee, which I thought meant he expected the wedding to go as planned. And that was good, considering my parents were leaving for Italy soon.

It was late, and Bo and I were hungry, so we headed home without Dylan. He said he'd be by later if he could get out before I went to bed, but I told him not to bother. I had some work to do, along with some last minute wedding planning stuff, but first, I wanted to add to my notes about my suspects.

Bo and I had a pattern and both of us settled right into it when we got home. He did a security walk around the backyard while I prepared his yummy grub, a new to us brand the vet recommended for his tummy. He was the kind of dog that, if something smelled, that meant it was edible, and a lot of what he ate wasn't, so soon after the consumption, his stomach regretted it. And that regret had anyone within smell shot suffering. I cared less that I suffered, because sometimes, if I was being honest, the sounds his little tummy made fascinated me, but I didn't want him to suffer, so we went with the brand the vet recommended. It hadn't stopped him from eating things that didn't belong in any stomach, but it had stopped the battle within it.

As he snarfed down his kibble, I prepared a small salad for myself. I tossed a little romaine lettuce, fresh tomatoes and some cucumber slices with a shake of parmesan cheese and a squeeze of lemon in my bowl and sighed. I missed salad dressing, but like Bo with his inedible findings, it didn't agree with my stomach.

We sat in the family room, Bo on the couch and me on the floor between it and the coffee table where I'd spread out the entire contents of my work bag.

I leaned my head back next to his on the couch cushion. "Do you see the irony here?"

He licked my face, which likely meant he didn't care. Good thing I didn't, either.

I added to each note card for Skip, Floyd, and Dabney.

Floyd and Dabney had thrown Carole under the bus like a discarded Coke can, and though Skip hadn't exactly done the same, he hadn't really done much of the opposite, either.

Floyd made a point of saying he couldn't cook, and specifically mentioned that he burned cookies in a class he'd taken, but unless I had the details on the class, I couldn't verify that. I made a note to ask for those details.

Dabney. I leaned my head back onto the couch again. "That woman makes me even more grateful for Belle."

Bo agreed by swiping his tongue along the side of my cheek.

"Thank you. I needed to get that old makeup off."

He did it again.

My cell phone buzzed. I stretched underneath the table where it had slid. I didn't recognize the number, so I let it go to voicemail, but shortly after, I received a text message from the same number.

"It's Skip Rockwell. Can you meet me tomorrow?"

I stared at the text message, wondering what he wanted, and why it required us to meet. I had a lot to do before heading to Italy, and not enough time to get it done, and I wasn't quite sure I wanted to meet with him without back up. "Is this something we can do over the phone? I can call you back."

He replied instantly. "Rather do it in person. It's important. I'll be at the Starbucks on Haynes Bridge and Old Milton at nine o'clock. Will that work for you?"

That was a busy area in Alpharetta, and he hadn't asked to meet somewhere private, which I wouldn't have done, so I assumed he didn't have anything nefarious planned. It would be hard to pull off a murder in such a public place.

Unless poison was his weapon.

I texted back that I'd be there, and promised myself I'd order my own coffee, and not let it leave my hands while there, just in case.

CHAPTER SIXTEEN

Dylan didn't make it over that night, and I went to bed shortly after detailing out my notes on the case and emailing the wedding manager about some final details. Before shutting off my computer though, I did take another peek at the location. We'd picked the beautiful castle Aragonese on the island of Ischia, a short ferry ride from Napoli, Italy. The weather would be perfect, or so said my special weather app, and the scenery stunning.

I couldn't wait for the big day, but I knew if I didn't get moving on everything else beforehand, I'd feel stressed the whole time we spent in Italy, and I didn't want that. So, that's what I did. I got moving on everything else.

I sent Belle a quick text to let her know what I was doing, and instead of stopping at Millie's, dropped Bo right at day care, and headed straight to Alpharetta. I took Interstate 400 but got off at exit fifteen in Cumming and hit the backroads the rest of the way. I didn't mind the drive, but I hated sitting in traffic, and that interstate was a constant parking lot from exit 14 into Dunwoody, if not farther, since it was the only option to the city from the north suburbs.

I'd texted Dylan, too, but he hadn't responded. I didn't exactly tell him where I was going or whom I planned to meet, but I did say I might have something for him later. I knew I behaved shady by doing that, but I also knew he'd either want to go with me, or try to stop me from going at all, and something told me I needed to go.

I blamed that gut he told me to listen to.

When I got out of the car, he called, and I felt bad for it, but I hit decline so I could get inside and talk to Skip without the lecture.

He was there sitting in a corner table when I walked in. "Let me get a coffee, I'll be right back."

I ordered my large Pike coffee with room for cream, filled it with the half and half on the counter, and took a seat across from him at the small table. "So, what's this about? The last time we spent alone together you threatened me."

He sighed and took a sip of his coffee. "I didn't intend to sound that way. I just wanted you off my back."

"So, what's changed?"

He did a quick review of the people in the small Starbucks and then whispered, "I didn't kill Carole, but I think whoever did has been watching me, and I think we both know who the killer is."

"Watching you?"

He nodded. "Here's the thing, Carole and me, we knew what Floyd and Dabney were doing. That's why she came to me. It wasn't her planning to leave first, it was Dabney funneling business to Floyd. When Carole figured it out, she approached me, and we made a deal."

"For her to move her business to you?"

He nodded again. "She was angry. Furious, actually, and she knew if she leaked a little information, word would get out, and the good agents would come over with her. That was the plan."

"Did she implement the plan?"

"She'd started, and Dabney must have caught on, because the next thing we knew, even more of the homes her clients wanted to make offers on suddenly sold to Floyd."

"Why would she come to your firm? I've been to both, and with all due respect, there's a big difference between yours and theirs."

He shrugged. "I asked her the same question. My son is always giving me grief because we don't have a detailed online marketing plan among other things. He's wanted to run it, but I'm more of a direct mail kind of guy. He's been trying to get me to get on that wagon for over a year now."

"He's not exactly wrong."

"I know. Carole convinced me of that. She had a solid online presence, and along with her client base, we both saw a big opportunity to merge. She wanted a fresh slate, something she could work with that wasn't hindered by a jealous, deceiving partner, and I needed to get with the times."

"Why not just use your son to do it? He seems like he'd know how it works given his age."

"I hadn't really considered it until Carole approached me. John's a great kid, and he's a strong seller, but he's got a lot of growing to do. He's not ready to be a partner, and he's definitely not ready to make major decisions. Needs more years under his belt. I figured if I can get the company to a level even close to Craddock & Clayton, I could retire and leave him my place in the company. That was my plan."

"And he's okay with that?"

"I haven't told him yet. He wasn't thrilled with Carole coming on board, and since she was killed, we haven't talked about what I'd planned. Haven't had a lot of time to do that now."

"I can understand." I tapped my foot on the ground. Again, I had that gut feeling I was missing something, I just didn't know what. "Why are you telling me this and not the sheriff?"

He glanced behind him again. "Like I said, I think someone's watching me. I'm afraid if I go to the sheriff, I'll end up in a bag at the morgue by the end of the day."

I understood his fear, at least in a generalized way.

"Have you heard of Rachel Hudson?" he asked.

"The food blogger from Atlanta? I'd think everyone's heard of her. She's all over social media and TV."

"We found out she's planning a big move to Alpharetta. She's planning to interview realtors next week."

"Okay?"

"John had this wild idea to take her cooking class last month. Thought if he did that, he'd build a relationship with her and get her business."

"Sounds like a solid plan in my opinion."

"He's a great cook already, and he wouldn't make a fool of himself, so I told him to go for it. And you know who was in the class with him?"

"Floyd Bowman."

He leaned back in his seat. "You got it."

"They made cookies. Floyd said he'd burned his."

"What would you expect him to say? He took that class, and then what happens? A woman ends up dead, from cookies."

"You were at the town meeting. My fiancé said it wasn't the cookies."

"No, the sheriff said the cookies in her *stomach* weren't the cause of her death."

"And before that, you mentioned that Carole was poisoned, but no one else knew that. The sheriff's office hadn't released that information."

"I may not have the big firm like Dabney and Floyd, but I'm not stupid, Miss Sprayberry. I did the math. Carole liked her sweets. Like I said, everyone knew that. If she'd been shot or something, your sheriff friend would have said. But he didn't. When it first happened, no one said anything about how she was killed, so I made an assumption that she was poisoned. Carole could have eaten a cookie days before she died. It didn't have to be the ones in her stomach when it actually happened."

"Where's your son?"

He blinked. "He's...he's got appointments this morning. Said he'd be back to the office later today. Why?"

"You stay put." I grabbed my phone and hit Dylan's cell short cut. "I'm serious, don't leave here until you hear from me." I stood and made a beeline for the door because I didn't want Skip Rockwell asking me any other questions.

CHAPTER SEVENTEEN

"Well look who's here, Lily Sprayberry. What're you doing in my neck of the woods?" John Rockwell leaned against my car in the parking lot of the strip mall where the Starbucks was located.

I held my phone against my hip and shut off the volume with the silence button on the side. "Funny seeing you here, John." I grabbed a hold of the strap on my bag to try and hide the fact that my phone was also in my hand.

He was too distracted by his ego to notice. "How about we go for a drive. I have this property to show you. It's up off 369 and Busbee Road. You'll love it."

I knew that property, and I also knew it was in an isolated area with nothing much but woods surrounding it.

He held his right hand at his waist, and that's when I saw the gun. "Come on, you drive."

As I walked over to the car, I quickly hit the short cut to dial Dylan's number. I prayed to God that Dylan had either answered his phone, or that his voicemail was recording our conversation. I'd long ago shared my location with Dylan through my GPS on my phone, and he'd once put a GPS tracker on my car, so I knew he'd be able to locate me. I just hoped he realized he needed to. I got into my car and quietly set the phone in the section of the door frame for odds and ends, speaker side up. I kept my bag over my shoulder, but John removed it and threw it in the backseat.

"Pull out on Haynes Bridge and make a left. We're going the back roads. It's a pretty drive."

"Your dad knows. He knows what you did."

He laughed. "My father wouldn't know a killer if one looked him in the eye. He's too dumb to sell homes let alone figure out the truth."

"I wouldn't count on that."

I hit the green light at Old Milton and Haynes Bridge and crossed through it. "Turn right up there." He waved his gun to point ahead.

"You wanted to be a partner in the firm, and when you found out Carole was coming on, you killed her."

He smiled. "You're not as dumb as that partner of yours now, are you?"

"Belle's not dumb. She was playing you. She laughed about it. We both did."

He growled. "That's bull, and you know it. I had her eating out of the palm of my hand."

Not only was John Rockwell a murderer, he was a delusional one at that.

"A few more days and she'll be crying on my shoulder for her dead friend."

I gripped my steering wheel tighter. "You plan on killing your dad, too? He knows someone's been following him, and he knows it's the killer."

"You don't have to worry your pretty little head about my dad."

He directed me onto a back road I didn't know.

"He wanted to improve the business for you. Did you know that? That's why he decided to partner with Carole. He said they'd build it up, and he'd retire and give you his half. He brought her on for you."

He flinched, and I knew I'd set him back with that, but then shoved the gun into my arm. "He brought her on because she's a moneymaker, and he's selfish. It had nothing to do with me."

"You're wrong. He told me it was all for you."

He laughed. "I could have done exactly what that woman was planning to do. He just didn't give me a chance. When I met with her and she laid out her plan, I laughed. My ideas were better than that snobby old woman. Who handles social media better, a middle-aged woman or someone our age?"

"That's not a reason to kill her."

"Sounds like a good enough one to me."

I drove ten miles under the speed limit, and John smacked my shoulder with the tip of his gun. "Faster. I got plans to stop by your office this afternoon. Your cute little partner is going to go out with me whether she likes it or not."

Over my dead body, I thought. I just hoped I wasn't actually right. I hit the gas and kicked up my speed to twenty over the limit, hoping that maybe an officer would be lurking on another back road and spot me.

That didn't happen though. When we arrived at the property, he forced me to pull into the gravel drive and get out of the car. My mind raced for a way to grab my phone, but he forced me out too quickly to even try.

"Over here." He shoved the gun into my back. "Use the lock and let us in."

"I don't have the code."

"4-2-6-0."

I unlocked the lock and entered the old home.

It had been vacant for years, and from what I knew, the old man that owned it had recently died, so his family decided to sell it without making any repairs or emptying the ratty furniture.

He directed me to the back room off the kitchen. "Stand there."

I stood to the right of center in front of a blue and burnt orange couch. On the table was a lamp without it's shade. I eyed it and scooted slowly over just a centimeter at a time.

"I'd be sorry about this, but I can't bring myself to feel bad. You deserve this, Sprayberry. Sticking your nose where it doesn't belong isn't a trait I like to see in women."

"How did you do it? How'd you kill her?"

He laughed, flipping his gun in a circle in his hand. "The woman was a freak for cookies. Probably had some kind of overeating issue or something, I don't know. I just helped her with that addiction. I met her the night before, you know, to discuss her worthless marketing plan, and I brought her two batches of cookies. Told her I'd had a change of heart and was happy she was coming on board. Said one batch was for her, and the other for a showing. Dumb woman was stupid enough to take a cookie from the first plate and eat it right in front of me. When she ate the second one, I had to stop myself from laughing." He smiled. "I knew she'd be dead before the next afternoon."

"John, no. How could you?" Skip Rockwell appeared in the entry way to the backroom.

John kept his gun pointed at me. "Get out of here, Dad. This doesn't concern you."

"Son, please. Don't do this. You have a future. The company. Starting a family. Don't ruin it. We can work this out."

John whipped around and aimed the gun at his dad's head. I dove to the side of the couch and grabbed the lamp, begging God it wasn't plugged in. I yanked and pulled it from the wall and screamed as I smashed it on top of John Rockwell's head.

It stunned him, but he didn't go down.

His father charged him and wrestled to get the gun, as I jumped on his back and punched his neck and head as hard as I could. The gun flew across the room, and the two of them dropped to the ground, crawling for it, with me still hanging onto John Rockwell's neck. I climbed off and charged for the gun, kicking it into the hallway on the second try.

And directly into Dylan's path.

He and a deputy held their guns drawn on both men.

"Freeze," the deputy said.

"Or don't. I'd be happy to shoot someone for messing with my fiancée and our wedding," Dylan said.

I smiled at him. "Glad you could make it today."

He smiled back. "Looks like the wedding's a go, Lily Bean."

Chapter Eighteen

The wedding did happen, though not exactly as planned. It went better than I'd ever dreamed it could have.

There were four additional guests on our flight, and they made a big deal about being in first class. The eight of us took up the first two rows on each side, and I felt for Pam and Staci, the flight attendants.

Henrietta sat with Old Man Goodson for the first half of the nearly twelve-hour flight, and since it was an overnight trip, she spent that time snoring louder than my dog.

Bo. How I wished he could have been with us. He would have made the perfect ringbearer.

Pam and Staci laughed every time they passed by, telling us stories of other flyers and their snoring habits. I showed them pictures of my favorite snorer, and as I did, Henrietta snored so loud she woke herself up.

Poor Old Man Goodson nearly had a heart attack, too, so Billy Ray did him a favor and switched seats.

"This won't mess up those special agents flying with us now, will it?" he asked. "I don't want people confusing me of being that old guy if the plane crashes."

"Sir," Pam said, "I promise you, in the unlikely event of something like that, the airline will do their best to properly identify your remains."

Billy Ray's jaw dropped, and the rest of us laughed.

Bonnie leaned out of her aisle seat and did not whisper to Pam, but spoke with clarity and volume, "Good thing he's a looker. The porch light's on, but ain't nobody home."

Pam giggled.

The two flight attendants showered us with treatment above what I'd expected in first class, including free champagne and fresh chocolate covered strawberries. When I thanked them, they both told me to thank the maid of honor, that she'd gone to great lengths to make the flight special.

I wondered what else she had up her sleeve.

When she stood and walked into the attendants' cabin area, I knew she had a plan.

Pam's voice came over the loudspeaker. "Ladies and gentlemen. We have some special guests on this flight today, and I'd like to share their wonderful news. Lily Sprayberry and Dylan Roberts sitting in seats one A and B, are heading to the island of Ischia to tie the knot."

The whole entire plane cheered, and Henrietta whistled loud enough to break the sound barrier, which concerned me because we were high enough in the sky that it could have happened.

"And to celebrate, their maid of honor and best man would like to do a toast."

Staci and two other flight attendants came out pushing carts.

"Champagne was donated by the Bramblett County Sheriff's Office deputies, but if you prefer sparkling water, or aren't old enough for alcohol, we've got that, too."

They handed out the drinks quickly, and Belle and Matthew said a wonderful toast that I hoped they'd written down because I didn't want to forget it.

Belle spoke first. "I'd like to take a moment to say it's about darn time these two tied the knot. God bless this man for courting my best friend with a swift and motivated attitude, because she is a hot mess, or was a hot mess in the love department."

We all laughed.

"But here's the thing, there's never been another man for Lily Sprayberry, or should I say Lily Roberts. No other man could handle her, and no other man could care for her heart the way Dylan has. I've been telling her that for years, and thank God he showed up back in town because otherwise she would have for sure ended up a spinster."

"Hey," I complained. "You don't know that for sure."

"Someone would a made a wife outta her," Billy Ray said, giggling.

"Honestly though, I am so glad they are together, and I'm so glad they finally made it official. My best friend deserves a good man, a man with a big heart, and the patience to put up with her. She's found that in Dylan. And you—" she held up her glass to my husband. "You hit the jackpot with this one, so remember that when she's sticking her nose where it doesn't belong, you hear me?"

He nodded. "Loud and clear, Belle. Loud and clear."

Matthew was next, and his speech made my eyes water.

"I haven't known the bride all that long, but I feel like she's family to me, and I hope she feels the same way. I've known her good for nothing husband here for a long time. Y'all think he's a good man, but you're wrong."

Dylan's mouth opened, but not in fear, more in sarcasm.

"He's a great man," Matthew said. "And he loves that woman more than any of you know. I spent many a night in Atlanta listening to him talk about the girl back home, the one that stole his heart, and the one that he regretted letting go. When he finally decided to move back to Bramblett County to win her back, I worried he couldn't do it, but now, watching them together after all this time, I know they were meant to be."

I nudged my husband. "I never knew."

He wrapped his arm around me. "My heart couldn't let you go, and I knew I had to get you back."

"I love you."

"Love you more."

The night went by in a flash, but not nearly as quickly as the wedding.

I wished I could savor every minute of it, and I tried, I did, but time sped up, and even though I appreciated the beautiful ceremony, it was just too darn quick.

One minute, Belle was fluffing my train before she walked the gorgeous white carpeted path from the stairs of the castle to the altar, and the next, Dylan was waking me up on our hotel bed, and I was still in my dress.

"How long have I been sleeping?"

"Three hours."

"Wow." I sat up and rubbed my eyes. "I can't believe I crashed like that."

"You've had a lot going on."

"You did, too."

He kissed my forehead. "You ready to finish the night, Mrs. Roberts?"

"I am, Mr. Sprayberry Roberts."

"Cute, but that's not on the marriage license."

"Are you sure?" I tossed on a casual pink and white striped sundress and pulled my hair into a ponytail. "An easy fix if it's not."

We walked into the lobby of the hotel and greeted our guests. The reception had been small, with just close family and those surprise friends, but we did all the traditional things even though I had to be gently reminded of a few, like the violin playing the right song for our first dance.

"I can't believe you didn't recognize it," Belle said. "It was clear as day."

"I had a lot going on. You just wait. If you ever get married, you'll understand."

"If I ever get married? Oh, I'm getting married, we'll just have to see who the lucky guy is."

Matthew raised his hand. "Pick me."

"Wait, is that a proposal?" Dylan asked. "Way to steal the spotlight."

Matthew grabbed Belle and pulled her close. "Let's just call it a bid for the job."

"You've got a lot of courtin' to do, big guy," she said.

"I'll give it my best shot."

Momma rushed over, her mascara bleeding down just under her eyes. She'd cried through the whole wedding, and even the quick reception. I took a tissue from my small purse and wiped the marks away.

"Oh honey, you looked just beautiful up there," she said. "I don't think I'll ever get that image out of my head."

"Well, just remember that when you hear something about me through the gossip train, okay?"

She laughed. "My momma always said a small-town's gossip was better than the nightly news."

Bonnie laughed. "Now we know how come Lilybit's always talking about her momma. She gets it from her."

"My momma always told me to keep my knees together and my mouth shut," Henrietta said.

Belle snorted. "I bet she was a hoot."

Henrietta shrugged. "Not as much as me."

I pulled Belle aside, and we walked over to the café at the start of the hill to the castle. "By the way, how did you get them here? The flight was expensive. They don't have that kind of money."

A man in a fedora and a three-piece suit sat at the head table with a line of men and women leading to him. Each person took a turn kissing the man's ring.

"What's up with that?" Belle asked.

I shrugged.

"So yeah, Dylan paid for their flights and their hotel rooms. It was his idea. I just set everything up. Made sure they were packed, got them to the airport, that kind of thing."

"Dylan paid for it?"

"Honey, looks like your husband's got a stash of cash you don't know about."

The sun set, turning the ocean a deeper blue and the sky a range of lovely burnt orange to various shades of purple.

It was pure heaven, just like I'd imagined.

Dylan and Matthew walked up with the four musketeers, and Bonnie didn't shy away from speaking her mind again. "What's all the fuss about that man's ring?" She wobbled over to him, and two large men in black suits immediately stood up and blocked her from even seeing the man at all. They said something in Italian, and a woman nearby grabbed a hold of Bonnie's arm and led her back to us.

"That's Raimondo Angelini. He's the Don. You no walk up to him without waiting in line." She shook her finger at Bonnie. "Is no good. Bad manners."

"What's a Don?" Bonnie asked.

Dylan pulled out the seat next to him. "Here. Sit." He helped her push in the chair.

I thanked the woman for rescuing our friend.

"A Don is the head of the mafia here. He's a big man in the community, and his position demands respect, even from tourists," Dylan said.

"That man's a criminal?" Billy Ray asked.

"Shh," I said. "You're going to get us killed."

"Should have brought the clubs," Old Man Goodson said.

"And the bats," Henrietta added.

My mother had just walked up then. "What would you need a bat for?"

"Please, don't," I begged.

But it didn't matter. Bonnie and the gang filled her in on their need to protect me, and Dylan and I spent an hour being lectured about my safety.

Momma even threatened to move back, and while I'd love to have my family around to visit more, I was excited to build my home with Bo and my husband.

Because that was exactly how things were meant to be.

THE END

Keep up with Carolyn and receive a free ebook at carolynridderaspenson.com

If you enjoyed this book, please leave a review on the site where you purchased it. Thank you.

ACKNOWLEDGEMENTS

Thank you to my wonderful editor, Jen, my favorite proofreader, JC Wing, my favorite beta reader, Lynn Shaw, Wilfrieda Schultz my PA, and my friends and family who've supported me as I've traveled along this writing journey.

If you like my work, please sign up for my newsletter at carolynridderaspenson.com and visit me at carolynridderaspenson, author on Facebook and carolynridderaspenson on Instagram!

Also, check out my wonderful author friends in our Sleuthing Women Author Collective on Facebook.

About The Author

Carolyn Ridder Aspenson currently calls the Atlanta suburbs home, but can't rule out her other two homes, Indianapolis and somewhere in the Chicago suburbs.

She is the bestselling author of the Angela Panther Mystery Series, The Lily Sprayberry Cozy Mystery Series, and the Chantilly Adair Psychic Medium Cozy Mystery Series.

MORE BOOKS BY CAROLYN

The Angela Panther Contemporary Mystery Series
Unfinished Business
Unbreakable Bonds
Uncharted Territory
Unexpected Outcomes
Unbinding Love
The Christmas Elf
The Ghosts
The Event
Undetermined Events
The Inn at Laurel Creek Contemporary Romance Novella Series
Zoe & Daniel's Story
The Inn at Laurel Creek
The Lily Sprayberry Realtor Cozy Mystery Series
Deal Gone Dead
Decluttered and Dead
The Scarecrow Snuff Out
Sleigh Bells & Sleuthing (A Holiday Author Novella Collection featuring Lily Sprayberry)
Signed, Sealed and Dead
Bidding War Break-In
Open House Heist
Realtor Rub Out
The Chantilly Adair Psychic Medium Cozy Mystery Series
Get Up and Ghost
Ghosts Are People Too
Praying for Peace
Author Shared Series

Mourning Crisis
The Funeral Fakers Series
Independent Novellas
Santa's Gift A Cumming Christmas Novella

Purchase Carolyn's books through the online retail
outlet where you purchased this one.

Printed in Poland
by Amazon Fulfillment
Poland Sp. z o.o., Wrocław